Requiem

Cassandra Frew

I0543514

This is dedicated to my wonderful critic who did
me the honour of reading these books in their draft
stages - my little dynamo, Di (aka Diane Julia
Harris, nee Golding). As with my other supportive
and wonderful friends, your names are forever
emblazoned via the character names here in print.
And, as always, to my late husband Chris.
Without your love and support, this series of books
would never have eventuated.

Commenced 22 February 2011
Completed 9 June 2016

Covers designed by Microsoft® Clip Art and used with permission by Microsoft.
Microsoft, Encarta, MSN, and Windows are either registered trademarks or trademarks of Microsoft Corporation
in the United States and/or other countries.

TABLE OF CONTENTS

PREFACE

AS WAS PREDICTED, Lorien became the stay-at-home Daddy and I had been working as the music teacher at Sommersett High as a casual since Alan O'Dowd retired.

I loved the job and Lorien loved being home with Mercy, although she did regular day-care. This was not only for her social development, but to allow Lorien some hours in the day to dedicate to his music.

He'd also finally won the pool table versus piano argument with his twin. With Elijah having less and less time due to his long and erratic doctor hours, he finally relented. Lorien had the pool table sold and a baby grand piano in pride of place within a month.

Our lives were full, rich and hectic but not much else had changed in our little world. The one exception was our Mercy had grown from a baby into a toddler, a toddler about to turn three...

FOUR...

The Party Favour

"She's the girl with the curls of brown
My little princess doesn't need a crown
And on your birthday, a full of mirth day
You'll shine like the sun, among the crowd."

L Standish, 'Three Times Three'

LIFE WAS GETTING CRAZY, with a capital K! Mercy was turning three and we were about to get what seemed 1,500 kids turn up for her party. There were already so many toys in the house, many of which she didn't even play with for more than five minutes before they were discarded. Lorien had bought so many more for her birthday under the guise of her understanding this year what was truly going on. Neither of the twins was worried about what had become our cramped living areas. 'Mercy's Tip' I now lovingly referred to our home, but I was just about at my wit's end. And, Christmas was right around the corner.

I was banished to the kitchen whilst the twins decorated the house and yard, opting to have the celebration on the verandah, being such a beautiful summer's day. The barbeque was already heating, and so was my frustration. As I added the last of the lollies to the top of the homemade cake, I burst into tears. I swiped at them angrily, knowing I was tired and more than a little annoyed with my beloved husband. I threw the spatula into the sink with a clatter and took to the stairs, seeking out the only sanity left in the house – our bedroom. *Just five minutes*, I thought to myself. *A quick nap to refresh me before they all get here.*

"Ash?" I heard whispered, and then the bed dipped, signalling Lorien now at my side.

"I just need a few minutes."

"Our friends are here when you're ready," he said, running his fingers lightly through my hair.

"I should get up then," I sighed, and swung myself into a sitting position next to him.

"Stay, get a nap," he said and leant in for a kiss. As the kiss deepened, Lorien laid me back down, one leg gliding effortlessly between my own.

"This is not napping," I mumbled through the kiss. His lips tightened against my own in a smile, and he drew back slowly.

"Sorry Baby," he muttered, grazing his lips softly over my brow and cheeks. I heard a drumming of feet in the hallway, then Elijah's voice,

"Mercy! No!" seconds before the door burst open.

"Orrie? Baaaaaaaby?" Mercy called as she came through the door, Elijah hot on her heels.

"How's my birthday-Bump?" Lorien asked as she crawled onto his lap for hugs and kisses. Elijah looked at me and grinned. He knew how long I had been *trying* to get her to call us Mummy and Daddy, but like a mynah bird, she repeated everything verbatim. I had been fortunate with a smattering of 'Mummy's', especially when she wanted something, but so far Lorien had not once been referred to as Daddy. I think it worried me more than him.

Lorien got his kiss and cuddle and then she clambered over to me. I hugged her and tried to explain it again. "Daddy calls me 'Baby', you call me Mummy, just as you call Daddy, 'Daddy', not Lorien. That's what adults call him." She grinned up at me and reconfirmed,

"OK Mummy!" I laughed and kissed her on the cheek before putting her back on the ground and giving her little bum a pat. "What about Unkie Lie?" she asked holding onto one of his legs, looking up at him.

"Unkie Lie is right on the money, Honey," he verified for her, and swept her into his arms. "Come on Merce; let's give Mum and Dad a few minutes of privacy." That was another thing - she was in the process of learning to knock.

I went to follow them out and Lorien stopped me, pulling me back to sit next to him on the bed. His hands caressed lovingly across my stomach. I raised my eyes to meet, what I expected, a sly expression in his own. I was surprised to find a gleeful twinkle instead, causing me to ask, "What?"

"Do you think you might be pregnant Baby?" he asked with a smile.

"Ah, ahhh," I stammered, not having thought about it. Lorien was always more on top of these things than I. "I don't think so..." I didn't feel pregnant.

"I'll get a test tomorrow."

"If it makes you happy Honey."

"It will make me ecstatic if you are," he said and drew me in for another soft kiss.

When his fingers sought out the buttons on my shirt, I slapped lightly at his hands. "Orrie, no!" I warned. He laughed and sat up, hugging me against him. "We're about to have a house full of kids, possibly another one inside me, and all you can think about is your dick!" I admonished playfully.

"My dick," he scoffed. "It's *our* dick, Baby."

"Well then, put *our* dick away for now."

"For now?" I smiled back at him, definitely only for now...

Michael, Glen, Bree and Simon were out on the verandah with a few of the kids who had arrived whilst we were upstairs. Mercy was already hooting it up and they were all excited. A small pile of presents was stacked on the table, waiting for the opening ceremony to commence sometime later. Elijah, having given them all a drink from the esky, was currently in the process of explaining some rules when the doorbell rang again. Elijah went to get it, leaving Lorien and I to greet our friends.

After a quick exchange of kisses, I went back into the kitchen to start bringing out round one of the party food. Entrée: lollies, chips, chocolate crackles, fairy bread, cocktail frankfurts, pigs in a blanket, mini pizzas and devilled eggs. The latter three were primarily for the adults, not thinking the kids would like the eggs, but I was surprised to see them gobbled down regardless. With some chagrin, I imagined having to hose off the jumping castle that afternoon.

The last kid was dropped off just after 1.00 pm and the party started in full swing. We let them run wild at first, saving the games for when they needed a break.

I had noted through the childcare books that kids are lumped into one of three categories: flexible, fearful and feisty. And sure enough, here was the child clinging to his 'blankie'; the loud, overbearing screamer and thankfully, the flexible ones like our Mercy. I was starting to wish that we had allowed the parents to stay, as was the norm these days. I still didn't relish the idea of catering for adults as well as kids, other than my adult friends of course. I now had to live with my decision and the aftermath. "Lorien, go and break that up will you," I said, and he swivelled his head, catching my inference. Blanket boy was currently cowering in a corner of the backyard whilst the screamer was running circles around him, Indian-whooping it up. The oddest part of this scenario was the bucket of pegs the screamer had over his arm.

"I wanna go home! I WANNA GO HOME!" Blanket-boy had found his voice.

"Pegs?" I heard Lorien mutter as he went to intervene. I smiled at him and he leant in to kiss me before going to organise 'pass the parcel'. Elijah went with him.

"Bet you can't wait to have more, hey Ash?" Michael drawled as he moved onto the seat Lorien had vacated. Was Michael psychic? Was I emanating pregnancy waves?

"Yeah, seven or eight would be great," I answered in obvious sarcasm. I leant over and dragged the esky toward me, removing all the red coloured drinks. This was one additional extra they didn't need playing havoc in their systems. There was enough sugar and crap on the table already without them.

Mum and Dad arrived around 2.00 pm and we decided to get the cooking started, giving Dad the job of tending the barbeque. He was happy with this arrangement; it meant he wasn't involved in keeping the kids entertained. "Kids! Lunch!" I called when the last of the snags were off the hotplate.

Gobble, gobble, gobble. If we were in the USA, it would have been Thanksgiving with all of that gobbling! However, it did seem to give them a slight lowering of the vitality levels, and the adults had a brief sigh of relief. All except Michael and Glen - they took the opportunity to use the empty jumping castle for a bit of their own childhood regression. "Hey!" yelled out peg-boy, pointing at Glen and Michael, Michael in the midst of a somersault whilst Glen looked on, laughing it up. They were having a good time!

"They can use it whilst you kids aren't on there," Lorien said and turned back to watch the action.

"They're too heavy!" he insisted.

"It will be fine," I assured him, and gave Mum a nod, signalling to go and get the cake. May as well get this over and done with now.

Elijah and Lorien had done their best to bring in the tradition of licking icing from a beloved's cheek by the birthday person. Although I had allowed this, against my better judgement, for Mercy's first and second birthday, I had warned them that it was to stop this year. She would remember it from this birthday onwards and having two male children living in the house was bad enough without the need to add another.

Michael and Glen joined us, breathless from their hijinks, for the cutting of the cake. Every eye of every child had been upon them when on the jumping castle, and this was still the case as they took a seat at the table. Mercy was the only one who wasn't surprised by her Uncle's monkey business; she had seen it before. It was hard not to laugh at some of the kid's faces. I doubt they had ever met anyone like Michael and Glen before; so happy to play with children's toys. It had kept them quiet though. "What are you smirking at woman?" Michael asked with a grin on his face.

"You!" I said and laughed. The kids all laughed with me, albeit that forced loud laugh when they don't really get what's funny. *I love you*, I mouthed to Michael. He blew me a kiss and mouthed back, *I love you morer!* And with that, the cake was placed on the table; three jaunty, fat candles waited for the breath of our girl to extinguish them.

"Yay!" all the kids chorused as Mercy blew, and then she screwed her eyes shut tightly, making her birthday wish.

"Know what I wished for Orrie?" she asked, climbing onto Lorien's lap.

"You're not supposed to tell me," he answered, tucking her hair behind her ears.

"But I must!" Lorien and I shared a smile. We never got over her dramatic choice of words at times.

"Well then, you had better tell me I suppose."

"I wished I could open my presents now!" Lorien laughed and put her back onto her feet, heading over to the table stacked with presents, pulling it closer to where we were sitting. Bree got up and disappeared inside the house, Michael followed her. I wondered where they were going. Elijah had the camcorder in his hands, so it wasn't for that reason.

They resurfaced a few minutes later, whilst Mercy was still in the midst of opening her first gift. Bree was dressed as a clown, complete with the white pancake makeup, pink wig, baggy pants, suspenders and huge shoes! "Happy birthday Mercy!" she called, and Mercy looked up surprised, her mouth forming a silent little O.

"Aunty Bree?" she asked, a little unsure. Bree nodded and put a finger to her mouth, making Mercy understand not to mention it. Mercy offered a huge grin and climbed onto her lap, taking star position for Bree to hand her the rest of her gifts. As each one was opened, Michael handed the accompanying card to me so I could note what came from each child. Mercy was expected to send thank you cards to all the guests. Well, Lorien and myself in her stead. She couldn't write more than her name at the moment.

What a haul! Among the myriad of gifts included Thomas the Tank Engine DVDs, Barbie dolls – both mermaid and Christmas Barbie, a silver locket, picture books, colouring books and pencils, a craft box full of little bits and pieces that I knew I would be vacuuming up in the not too distant future, and an assortment of games and educational toys.

All of a sudden, blanket boy started to cry. "What's the matter?" I asked as I went to console him, ensuring peg-boy was nowhere near. I wrongly assumed he was the culprit. I had an uneasy feeling that I didn't like that child, and felt guilty about it. I also felt guilty by thinking of them in pseudonyms and not their actual names. There were, however, quite a few kids here with the same name, so it did make it easier.

"She got the same gift from me and Rhiannon!" he cried, grabbing at my legs and pushing his face into me.

"Shhh," I soothed, "that doesn't matter." It did make Mercy take more notice of the pile in front of her, realising there were two identical Thomas DVDs in front of her.

"Here, he can have it back," Mercy said, tossing it over the table towards me. I don't think she meant it unkindly, but the reaction from Noah, aka blanket-boy, was immediate.

"She doesn't like my present! I want it back, I want it back!"

"OK, you can have it back," I assured him, giving Mercy the eye, letting her know what she had done was rude.

"I'm sorry Noah," she said, coming to us and hugging him from behind. "I do like your present." My heart melted every time our girl did something so selflessly. Noah chose to push her away, all achieved without moving his face from my leg.

"Now there is no need for that Noah," I said and looked up, hoping to find some adult support around to help me in this situation. Bree and

Michael had disappeared back inside, and Glen, Elijah and Lorien looked at me with massive grins on their faces. I shot them all a threatening glance, and as Lorien rose to mediate, Mum came to assist.

"How about we put your DVD with your things, and if you want to take it home when you leave, you can," Mum tried. Noah looked up at her, eyes swollen and red.

"I want it back," he muttered one more time before wiping his nose on my skirt. Great!

"Well then, you shall have it back," Mum beamed at him, attempting to get Noah to replicate her sunny smile. It worked. He took Mum's outstretched hand and followed her inside to help him get cleaned up.

It was getting hot in the backyard, and with a truckload of kids with full tummies, decided now was a good time for the sprinkler to go on. A bounce on the castle would no doubt see my earlier vision of hosing it down come to fruition.

We lined them up and sun-screened them; the Bananaboat aerosol was the *best* invention for a parent. With it suitably applied and stripped down to their swimmers and rashies, they were off. Elijah followed, using the portable music system to instigate a game of 'freeze!' when the music stopped. Hopefully this would prevent any further outbursts of 'not playing nicely together'. The sun hats and rashies did make it hard to tell one child from the other.

I glanced at my watch; it was just after 3.30 pm. Another hour and a half and it would be finished. "Baby, come to me," Lorien said, and I took my favourite position, on his lap. "Getting the better of you?" he asked, drawing my head to his shoulder and running his hand soothingly over my hair.

"Next year, we will let McDonald's be the host," I said, making him laugh.

"Nearly over," Michael said. "Then the adult party can start." They were all staying the night, voting to get through the first bout of birthday to then continue on with our reward for doing so. This was more Michael's idea than anyone else's but we were all in agreement. It was not going to be a childfree home though, two of Mercy's friends, who were also sisters, were staying the night - Jade and Jaimie. They were great kids, so would not be an issue. The adults would maintain the frivolity though.

Elijah's laughter cut through our table conversation and we all looked up to see the source of his outburst. Nothing exceptional was happening, but he was laughing, nonetheless. He called out over the music, "Listen to what they are singing!" Elijah had chosen Christmas music, as it was rapidly approaching, and the kids were all wrongly singing,

"I wish I was Mary Christmas, I *wish* I was Mary Christmas..." It cracked us all up. Kids!

At about a quarter to five, the Mums and Dads started to arrive to collect their little ones. They stayed and chatted for a while, before getting their child and lolly bag, thanking us for babysitting for the afternoon. I was amazed that Noah was now crying into his mother's lap, "I don't wanna go home, I DON'T WANNA GO HOME!" From one extreme to another, it would seem, but he and his family left shortly thereafter, Thomas DVD tucked under his arm.

Our neighbour from three doors down, and mother of Jade and Jaimie, was the last to arrive. Although her girls were staying the night, their older brother Caleb was going home. "God, you look frazzled," she said, taking the pineapple Cruiser from my outstretched hand. Jenny was a great neighbour and friend and we often had an afternoon of coffee, or had our kids staying overnight at each other's.

"It's been a long day," I admitted.

"Mine were OK?"

"Always, Jenny," I said and smiled. Her three kids then spotted her and came running to greet their mother with hugs and kisses.

"We're staying tonight?" Jade asked.

"Yes."

"Me too?" Caleb asked hopefully. More often than not, he was here with his sisters when they stayed.

"No, tonight it's just you, me and Dad." He pouted, his bottom lip starting to quiver. *It's OK, Caleb can stay too*, I mouthed to Jenny. "How about you all come and stay at our place tonight instead?" Jenny looked at me and I shrugged my shoulders, it wasn't a problem for me. However, it was Mercy's birthday and she needed to make that decision. She may not want to be away from her family tonight. That issue was solved quickly.

"Oh Mummy, can I?" she asked, loving the sleepovers at anyone's place.

"It's up to you Merce," I told her, and she grabbed Lorien's hand, tugging on it to get him to follow her.

"Where are we going?" he asked.

"I need to pack!"

Jenny and the kids ended up staying a while longer, eating more barbeque with us. At around 7.00 pm, they left, with Mum and Dad following shortly behind them. "We will let you get on with the rest of the party," Dad said with a smirk and Lorien and I walked them to the door. We both got a hug.

When I returned to the verandah, I poured a glass of champagne from the esky and flumped into a chair. Lorien took it straight back off me. "What?" I complained.

"Come with me."

"Lorien, what…" I continued, as he led me up the stairs toward our room.

"Just give me a minute, we need to talk."

"Can't you wait until we go to bed?" I asked, laughing.

"It's not about that," he tsked as we reached our room.

I sat on the bed and looked up at him expectantly, waiting on him to speak. "Do you think you should be drinking if you might be pregnant?" I had forgotten about our earlier conversation.

"I really don't think I am, Sweetheart."

"But, what if you are wrong?" He knelt in front of me and took my hands, letting me chew over his words.

"I'll just have a couple, OK?" He wasn't thrilled with my decision, but let it go.

"I know one way to slow the intake down," he purred, climbing onto the bed next to me, lowering me back into a kiss. I laughed and let him have his way. Sex with Lorien was better than any alcohol could ever be.

They weren't idiots; they knew what we'd been doing. It was obvious as we joined them on the verandah again, twenty minutes later. "God twin, you just can't keep it in your pants, can you?" Michael joked.

"Nope!" was Lorien's short reply. My tell-tale blush confirmed Lorien's answer.

We certainly didn't do it two or three times a day like we used to, but more often than not, our sexual interludes were still daily, or at the very least, every second day. You'd think by now we would have become stagnant, thrown a little more 'robotic action' into the fray, just going through the motions. But no, each and every single occasion was still brimming with arousal, heat and passion. It made me ache for him, my head swim with his scent and the feel of him. He assured me he felt the same way, and it was obvious. What had we done in a past life to deserve such bliss? We were the luckiest couple in the whole, wide world, and we knew it, thankful of the totally encompassing love we had for each other. It didn't appear that was ever going to change. We didn't want it to.

Having a three year old certainly cooled things off, however. So many times we'd been 'busted', but she was still too young to know what she had burst in on. It wouldn't be that way forever though and we considered putting a lock on the inside of our bedroom door. I argued that she needed to learn respect for other's privacy; Lorien's point was simply that he didn't have that much time, and just wanted to know we'd be uninterrupted. I had won eventually, and the lock stayed off. I couldn't bring myself to lock our child out of our room, especially when she would crawl in with us during the early hours of the morning if she had seen a monster under her bed. Lorien asked her recently how she knew there was a monster under her bed and her reply was "I can see his feet sticking out."

A Monster Spray was invented for her to use whenever she needed to banish them, and it had kept her in bed. Lorien was so with it sometimes, and the spray was harmless water in an atomiser bottle. The memory made me laugh. "Funny?" Lorien asked, taking my hand and drawing me to his lap. I shook my head, dismissing the thought.

It was like old times. We could have been 16 years old, except for the alcohol and joints, which of course Uncle Glen usually carried with him. I didn't partake, and neither did Lorien. "Don't feel like it," was his simple reply when I asked. Fair enough.

I sat there quietly, Lorien's lips to my nape, taking in the love I had for my funny friends. Elijah was the most festive of them all, regaling us with stories from the medical practice, ensuring he referred to no specific names. "No date tonight?" Simon eventually asked him.

"It is my niece's third birthday party, why would I bring a date?"

"To get laid," was Simon's blunt response. This cracked them all up and Elijah smirked, reaching for the near-empty snack tray. The munchies had set in. I stood, heading for the kitchen and the remains of the cake. This would prove most popular with the guests, and indeed, it was.

Satisfied for now, Michael looked pensive. This was not a good sign. As if in silent acknowledgement of my thoughts, he looked at me and smiled. "Time for a game?"

"What kind of game?" I asked suspiciously, narrowing my eyes at him.

"A normal game, of course," he huffed. "Monopoly, 80s Trivia, Uno... you know the sort." His eyes glinted in the half-light and I assumed there was more to come.

"What about poker?" Simon asked, "We haven't played that in years." Poker it was, and Bree went inside to grab the cards and poker chips. They made themselves at home, which was great. Neither Elijah,

Lorien nor I felt we had to play host and it certainly wasn't expected. Mi casa es su casa, and all that.

Michael shuffled the cards in his usual ripple effect and as he went to deal them out, he paused. "There's one catch."

"Of course," Lorien laughed.

"It's strip poker."

"Michael, why does it always have to be strip?" I groaned.

"I can't think of one instance we have *ever* played a strip game. Your twin is usually stripping you off in front of us."

"What about mine and Elijah's first date – you nearly had Lorien naked at Bree's place!"

"Nearly," Michael said, winking at Lorien. This time Elijah laughed, then smiled at me warmly, thinking back to the day and how much we had meant to each other. We still meant so very much to each other, but now, in an innocent family-orientated way. I smiled back.

"I'll protect you Baby, like on *our* first date." Lorien quietly interrupted. A surge of heat raced through me, thinking back to *that* day. Glassread baths, Lorien stripping me down and surrounding me with his body until I slid into the water. I turned to look at him and he was already leering mischievously at me. "Want to go to bed?" he whispered in my ear and I nodded, feathering my lips to his.

"Knock it off!" Michael called, "Let's get one of you nekkid first." I glared at the rest of them; they did not intend to argue against Michael's idea. "Now," Michael started as he dealt the cards, "the rules are a shot with each non-winning hand and a removal of one piece of clothing. Jewellery doesn't count," he added for Bree's benefit, who was currently waggling her fingers, showing off the numerous rings and bracelets. She immediately excused herself and returned a few moments later, wearing a few more layers of clothes.

"Thanks!" I huffed and she threw me a T-shirt of Simon's and a baseball cap. "Thanks!" I repeated, now in a more relieved tone.

"Hey, they're mine!" Simon called, grappling with Bree over the hoodie she had put on over her clothes. She stopped him with a soft kiss to his pouting mouth. "Well, OK then," he agreed and kissed her properly.

"God, now you two are starting," Michael tsked, pointing to the cards lying in front of us. "Come on!"

I wasn't sure if the guys were throwing their hands or not, but it wasn't long before Bree and I were still 90% clothed and they were down to their shorts. From where I was sitting, they all looked 'nekkid' already. And, of course, they were getting drunker with each loss, considering the shot that accompanied the strip. I supposed that would make it harder to win after downing a few shots of Schnapps.

Glen brought out another joint and Lorien had some this time. It also took the game in a blindingly fast new direction. Within five minutes, they were all now in boxer shorts or jocks. I had lost only the cap and a sock, and Bree the hoodie. I assumed we were going to get through this OK, but malevolently waited for the guys to drop like flies... one by one...

And, through poetic justice, Simon was first. He took great pleasure in turning his back on us and slowly sliding his jocks down. "Jesus Simon," Elijah laughed; he was sitting directly opposite him. Simon turned and sat quickly, throwing the jocks at Elijah who batted them away with the back of his hand. They landed on the grass and Michael jumped up, setting the cigarette lighter to them. They glowed briefly before the arc of embers fanned quickly across the nylon, turning it to ash. The elastic in the waistband was all that remained. We all sat there with mouths agape, hardly believing what we had seen. Simon broke the silence with an uproarious laugh, which got us past the shock and into the merriment. Michael; trust Michael!

But Michael was next, and I was amazed to see him remove his boxers without rising from his chair. My! How demure of him, and so unlike Michael. Bree called him on it though and he shrugged it off, collecting the cards and handing them to Glen for the next deal. "I'm going to throw this one," Lorien whispered, and I laughed.

"Haven't you already done that a few times?" I asked cheekily.

"Maybe once or twice," he said and wrapped his arms around me tighter. "Lucky I have my shield." But, he was true to his word.

I climbed off his lap and turned to face him, wondering how he was going to master this move. He stood unashamedly, dropped his boxers and pulled me back onto his lap. He grinned over my shoulder at the others, who were laughing. "You seem to be sitting a little higher Ash," Glen said, taking the amusement into hilarity. Lorien joggled me up and down as he laughed below me. Seconds later, the strength of him, on which I was sitting, was evident. One finger traced the side of my breast lightly, whilst the other drew the hair away from my neck, his lips finding my nape. And then we were up!

Lorien held me aloft in his arms and kissed me lightly. He looked at me, but spoke to them, "We're going to bed." The bow of my body in his embrace had covered him nicely, and he walked jauntily past them, knowing his bare arse was about to be on display to them all. He laughed softly into my mouth as the ensuing hyena-like reaction followed us up the stairs. They were smashed.

For good measure, he stopped part way up the stairs and put me back on my feet, kissing me with more force, leaving himself on display.

The background noise became a dull hum; all I thought about now was Lorien and his nakedness pressing so solidly against me. My hands slipped down his sides and over his tight rear, unasked. This was met with whistles and catcalls, but I was past caring. Lorien gave his rump a saucy shake, then drew away from me to turn toward them and bow. He was shameless, but considering his size, he had nothing to hide, although hiding it *would* be difficult. I still couldn't believe he had faced them with a full-blown erection. I did hear a muted 'holy shit' but was uncertain from whom it had come. It didn't sound like Bree… I then dragged him to our room. "Oooh Baby," he growled, noting my intensity.

With the bedroom door closed behind us, Lorien was set in motion, pressing me firmly against the wall from behind. He planted a few feathery kisses to my nape, and I spun around, forcing my body against his, grating my hips against his, to gauge the evidence of his arousal. His tongue parted my willing lips as my fingers traced over his strong arms, caressing at the pronounced ridge of muscle. He pulled me closer, travelling his hands down to roughly cup my rear, wrenching me forward for a deeper, more intense kiss. I let my fingers slowly glide down over his abdomen, carefully avoiding contact with his raging erection, when he stopped me and abruptly pulled away.

He smiled down at me, maintaining the slight distance from me, then slowly dipped his head, pausing to hover millimetres from my lips, so close that I could feel his warm breath. My entire body was throbbing, aching to be touched, and then he kissed me again, drawing my lower lip into his mouth and sucking on it lightly. I was so aware of the pulsating ache in my nipples, and I wanted him to kiss them the way he was kissing me.

I slipped a hand down and closed my fingers around his stone temple, making him groan through clenched teeth. "Very nice," he murmured appreciatively. Encouraged by his reaction, I worked it slowly, noting the twitch now within it. I leant forward and nuzzled into Lorien's neck, sliding my tongue up to his ear, in which I gently exhaled. His breathing was in rhythm with my own, his shoulders taut with tension.

Lorien kissed a trail down my collarbone, leisurely snaking his hands upwards, deliberately moving at a slow pace so that he could watch my eyes as I reflexively arched my back, pushing my breasts forward. But the time for games was over, and without warning, he grabbed my breasts and lightly squeezed them, eliciting from me a loud cry. He silenced me with his lips, stroking my nipples as he did so, and I squirmed in response. He continued to tweak a screaming bud as his other hand wended down to tease within my velvet folds. As he drew his finger through my slickness, he whispered, "You are so wet for me." I looked up into his deadpan eyes and nodded; his finger then delved within me and I could wait no longer.

"How do you want me?" I flustered, fumbling with my own clothing, wanting him inside me.

"Arse up." I crawled onto the bed and Lorien climbed on behind me, shifting to his haunches. He pulled my hips up high and glided himself through me slowly, coating himself in my arousal. He exhaled in a whispering laugh and I knew he was aware of how much I was burning for him, always so obvious. He drove into me from that high angle, the hard force taking me almost instantly over the edge. His 'tes-tickle-ers' hammered against my sensitive jewel and I threw my head back. Lorien grasped my shoulder with one hand, keeping me upright, as the other wended into my hair. My hands clutched the sheets tighter as he thrust with increasing urgency. My hips beat in time to his rhythm and my moans rose in syncopated chorus.

I could hear his gasps become more frantic, and then his body weight shifted slightly as he aligned his lips to my ear, hissing, "Come for me." He didn't have to ask twice, his coarseness ripping the last lucid thought from my head. Stars swam across my vision as my back arched, my face biting into the pillow to stifle a scream.

"Oh fuck Ash..." he groaned and stiffened, then shuddered, finding his own release. I forced myself back onto him as hard as I could and flexed my muscles, feeling every inch of him.

Lorien only smiled at me as he rolled onto his back, a loud sigh emitting from his lips, still curled into a grin. He kissed me as I luxuriated in the warm afterglow, the orgasm having left my limbs like jelly. I struggled to stay awake, the fingers of sleep creeping into my consciousness. Lorien brushed the hair from my forehead and kissed softly there, as my eyes fought to stay open. The last thing I remembered before falling into the abyss of sleep was the caress of his fingertips drawing patterns over my forearm.

Christmas

> *"Merry Christmas Baby!*
> *Come here, stand near*
> *No closer now, please Baby."*
>
> L Standish, 'You're My Mistletoe'

IT WAS HOT. The hottest summer I could remember and thankfully I wasn't 'with child' in this current climate. The pregnancy test had proven negative.

Mercy and I were sitting on the back lawn in our swimmers, occasionally making a break for the sprinkler when the cold trickle of our previous romp-through started to evaporate. "Whew!" Mercy said, flumping down next to me. "I think my sweat is sweating!" When I burst out laughing at her comment, she looked at me strangely. She had no idea of how funny she could be with her statements. Truly – out of the mouths of babes...

Lorien arrived shortly thereafter, a load of wrapped presents under his arm. "Hi Mummy," he said and leant down to kiss me.

"Oh! For me?" Mercy called, reaching for the closest gift, still in her father's arms.

"Not until Christmas Bump. Hands off for now!" Lorien answered. "Want something to drink ladies?" Lorien asked as he got to his knees, then stood, about to take the packages inside the house. Mercy and I both nodded.

On his return, he carried a lemon cordial for Mercy and a beer each for us. No sooner than he had sat down, Elijah came around the corner. "Man, that looks good," he said, taking off his jacket and mopping his face with a handkerchief. Lorien handed his brother the beer and went to get another. Such a wonderful connection they had. Elijah smiled at me and took a swig, then turned his attention to Mercy. "So Merce, did you go and see Santa today?"

"Yes, and he told me I had been a good girl this year." Santa had actually said no such thing, but she was about to extol to her Unkie Lie all the wonderful ideas of Christmas brimming inside her head. She was so excited.

"And did you sit on Santa's lap?" Mercy squidged her face up for a few seconds, puzzled, then replied,

"No, I sat on his knees." Elijah and I both laughed loudly, explaining the comment to Lorien as he returned, mid-mirth. "Stop laughing!" Mercy shouted, getting to her feet, hands on hips. As a rule, I would quell this outburst, but I did feel sorry for her. She had no idea what we were laughing at, and was obviously hurt by the confusion.

"It's OK Mercy," I said, and drew her to me, squatting her down on my lap. "It just sounded a little bit funny to us; you are funny sometimes without even knowing it. That is because we're adults and say things differently than you do. We're laughing because you make us happy, not because you said something silly." She looked at me dubiously for a moment then smiled, hugging her little wet body against mine. Such a sweet gesture, but the dampness on both of our bodies was starting to steam, and I was hotter than ever. "Want to hop back under the sprinkler?" I suggested. The boys stripped down to their boxers, and we all stood under the gentle geyser, letting it soak us to the skin.

When back in the shade, watching Mercy continue to romp under the spray, I shared with them the most embarrassing moment I had ever encountered. Whilst Mercy had been perched on Santa's lap, she lovingly stroked his beard, mesmerised by it. "You have lovely whiskers Santa," she told him. To which Santa smiled and thanked her. "Mummy has whiskers down there," she reported, pointing first at me, and then at her crotch. The twins burst out laughing.

"I would have loved to have been there," Lorien said. "It has been a while since I have seen that lovely blush."

"Blush!" I snorted. "Try bruise-purple."

"What are you laughing at?" Mercy asked, now back at our sides. Curiosity got the better of this cat all the time. We all looked at each other and burst out laughing again. She was not impressed, but how could I explain it to her. She would *not* have found it at all amusing!

The next day we decorated the house and put up the tree. Mercy had wanted to do it since early November, but we had managed to restrain her until after her birthday. The boys took care of the lights and outside decorations whilst Merce and I tackled the inside trimmings.

I draped rope tinsel over every available surface: the TV, curtain rods, lampshades, you name it, finishing off by winding it up the handrail of the staircase.

The tree took a little more time and effort. Mercy claimed one side, and I the other and we met in the middle. Strings of lights first, then the thousand or so ornaments, followed by the angel-hair tinsel. Mercy was humming to herself as she worked, and I hummed along with her. We were having a wonderful time. "I'm done!" she exclaimed, and came around to my side of the tree, plonking herself on my lap. "Ooooh, pretty!" she exclaimed, reaching up to touch the tinsel with a gentle finger. "Mine doesn't look as good," she pouted.

"Now, now, Mercy, there is no need for perfection." I stood and took her hand, walking to the other side of the tree.

It was hard not to laugh, but I knew I mustn't. I hadn't thought of her size, and due to the lack thereof, all the decorations were clustered around the bottom of the tree. The angel-hair was a clump that looked as if it had been shot from a cannon. "It's pretty Mercy," I said, and she smiled broadly. It was nothing that couldn't be fixed later, or simply left as is. There were no rules when decorating a Christmas tree.

We made some lunch and took it out to the boys, both of whom were currently on the roof. "Lunch!" I called, and Elijah gave a final whack with the hammer before following his twin down the ladder.

"How's the inside look?" Lorien asked, taking a sandwich from the tray and nearly ingesting it whole.

"So very pretty, Orrie," Mercy answered for me.

"Daddy," he reminded her.

"Daddy," she parroted. "Daddy…?"

"Yes?"

"When can we see the lights?" she asked in her 'best little girl in the world' voice.

"Not until night-time comes, Honey," he said, giving her hair a ruffle.

"Want to see what Mummy and I did?" she asked proudly, reaching for his hand to lead him inside. Elijah and I followed.

They suitably 'oohed' and 'ahhed', flattering her attempts, and she beamed at us. I refused to meet either of their glances, as I knew the look on their faces would match my own. In the end, we decided to leave the tree alone, and placed it in the corner with half of my side and half of Mercy's showing.

As soon as the sun was down, we traipsed outside to see the light show. I was so impressed with the vision before me, not realising how many they had strung. The entire southern frame of the house twinkled with a million pinpricks of starlight, the windows were outlined in ropes of red and white neon and within them, illuminated cut-outs of Santa was attached to one window, and Frosty in the other. A nodding pair of reindeer stood on the front lawn, and massive antlers were on either side of the entry door. Icicles dripped in a decreasing flashing light from the gutters, and ropes of green and white transformed the steps, also to neon. It all looked so festive, and I realised I was looking forward to this Christmas more than I had since when I was a child. Knowing that Mercy understood what was going on this year possibly assisted that feeling.

Christmas morning came all too soon. I had the alarm set for 6.00 am, aware Mercy would be up and eager. However, I was wrong. When 8.00 am rolled around, I sat up, knowing our guests would be arriving in a few hours and there was still a lot to do. "Come on Lorien, we need to go and wake the sleeping beauty."

Mercy wasn't in her room, so we quietly opened Elijah's door. And there they lay together, Elijah and his mini-me; arms wrapped around each other, heads thrown back, mouths agape and a hint of a snore coming from each of them. Lorien disappeared and came back a few seconds later with the camcorder. It was the cutest thing I had seen in a long time. It was a shame to wake them.

Once Mercy was surrounded by a wall of discarded Christmas wrapping paper, I sorted through the nearest pile to get my opened presents and moved them to the dining room table, before heading to the kitchen. A full champagne breakfast with lobster mornay vol au vents were the first course of the day.

Since Cara and Nick had moved away, the three of us vowed to always make Christmas a special day. This year was no different, with Mum, Dad, Cara's brother and sister, Howard and Marie, and Marie's family, husband Steve, Peter, and the twins Casey and Julie, also joining us this year. The best part of this year though was visiting Cara and Nick in Mackay, leaving tomorrow afternoon. We would have a second Christmas Day with them on Boxing Day evening. But, we hadn't told Mercy yet.

Just shy of 11.00 am, the doorbell rang. Mum and Dad were the first to arrive, armed with another stash of presents, most of them being for Mercy. She dove at my parents, wrapping her little arms around first Mum, then Dad's legs. "Grandma, Grandpa!" she exclaimed, "Santa caaaaaaaaaaaaame!"

"Well of course he did Honey, you have been such a good girl this year," Dad answered for them both, shooting me a sardonic grin. I rolled my eyes and took some of the gifts from him, putting them onto the table. As Mercy led them to the Christmas tree to show them exactly what Santa had brought her, the doorbell rang again. Lorien answered it this time.

It had been so long since I had seen Marie, Steve and the kids, they having moved back to Sydney about four years ago to look after an ailing Howard. I noticed the feathering of grey at Marie and Steve's temples, reminding me we were all getting older, not just the seventeen year old twins and a now twenty-two year old Peter, standing before me. The girls would have been thirteen and Peter eighteen when we last met. Although Sydney was not that far away, Peter had joined the Armed Forces and had only just finished his term of service, and the girls had been away at boarding school. They were also not at our wedding, being such a small affair. "Where's Uncle Howard?" Elijah asked, breaking my reverie.

"He wasn't up to it," Marie answered sadly, taking first Elijah, then Lorien, and finally myself in her arms for a hug. The cancer was taking its toll and Howard's time was drawing near. With Cara, Marie and Howard being orphaned at an early age, her already small family was shrinking further. I guess it was now up to our generation to continue its growth. But, so far, only Lorien and I had added another member to the ranks.

Marie noted my wistful smile and hugged me again, patting me on the back with reassurance. Dad then stepped in, handing out drinks, lightening the mood. Even the girls were handed a small glass of alcoholic punch each.

The two sets of twins took over the kitchen this year, leaving the parents to enjoy the antics of their granddaughter and great-niece. Mercy loved the limelight and was always looking for a new and captive audience. This left Peter and I to set the table. I did love a festive place setting, and Peter's height was an asset in reaching for the good dishes from the china cabinet. It was great to catch up with him, although he became slightly embarrassed when our discussion turned to the twins eighteenth birthday and his attempt at trying to 'woo' me, as he now put it. I laughed about it though, recalling the memory. This seemed to relieve him a little and I wondered if it had been worrisome for him over the years.

At nearly three o'clock, we were all finally ushered to the table. The feast was about to begin. The turkey was crisp, brown and succulent, the baked potatoes and pumpkin golden, the cobs of corn and peas dripped in artery-hardening butter, the baby carrots oozed honey, and the gravy was thick and rich. Before saying our annual session of Grace, we cracked our crackers and adorned the silly traditional paper crowns.

Mercy wore hers with pride, like a queen. The jokes never got any better and the crap toys became crappier, but what was Christmas in Australia without this custom? Mercy ended up with all the plastic rings, whistles and magnifying glasses, whilst the adults read the hackneyed jokes between mouthfuls of the most scrumptious Christmas dinner.

The girls had the privilege of making the pudding this year, although no one had room for it after lunch. They both looked sadly disappointed. We each managed to squeeze in a few spoonfuls, the brandy custard being the final straw to pushing me over the top. As per every Christmas, I was now physically nauseated.

Needing to work off my bloated feeling, I bustled them all outside whilst I rinsed everything before stacking it into the dishwasher. Another family tradition would then kick in; the men would fall asleep on the lawn. I glanced out of the window, watching the girls playing with Mercy, helping her remove the boxing from the bubble blower and sidewalk chalk. As I went to close the dishwasher door and turn it on, hands slipped around my waist. "Shall we go and have a lie down Baby?" I turned to my randy husband and raised an eyebrow at him.

"You have *got* to be kidding! I think I would vomit all over you!"

"Lovely Ash," Lorien grimaced, "way to break a mood!" I laughed, and he smiled before leaning in to kiss me.

The clearing of a throat brought us back to reality. Mum had returned to make yet another batch of her prize-winning punch. I could never get enough of it, and the blend of ginger ale, lemonade, tropical fruit juice, and apricot nectar made it not too fizzy and not too sweet. The fresh mint and pineapple chunks gave it texture and the passionfruit pulp frozen as ice cubes kept it cold. Other than the cherry liqueur chocolates, mixed nuts and summer fruit consisting of apricots, plums and of course cherries, this played the grand finale of what I considered necessary items that *had* to be incorporated into every Christmas. It just wasn't Christmas without them!

Later that evening, Lorien climbed into bed and flicked on the TV whilst I sat at the laptop checking my emails. Junk, spam, so and so knows someone on Facebook - the usual crap. And, look at this! A bank in South Africa was holding $1,000,000 for me, as I was a lost beneficiary. Did they really think people were so stupid? I highlighted them all and was about to hit delete when one in particular caught my eye. I unchecked it, deleted the rest and then re-read the email address and title line. It was from *muzakman* and the title read, 'This is not spam, open for a surprise, beautiful.' I made sure there was no attachment filled with a flesh-eating virus, or at worst, one that would screw up my hard drive, and decided to open it. I knew it could be unsolicited porn or some troll looking for cheap thrills, but admitted to myself they had appealed to my vanity. It read:

I have seen you walk by so many times, and my pulse races at the sight of you. You have captured my heart. Your smile lights up my world and your laughter fills me with a joy I knew not existed. You are the woman that Heaven has made for me, and even though you don't know who I am, I have, and always will, worship you from afar. Each day that passes makes my love for you grow stronger, and although I know we are not together, nothing can keep us apart forever. Not even the fact that you are with another. My desire for you will continue to grow across this distance, over any mountain, across any sea. Nothing can stand between you and I, nothing will stop me from meeting you. You are my future, and nothing will keep me from achieving my destiny.

This absolutely *reeked* of Lorien; I had no doubt about that. Between his enchanting lyrics, not to mention a few years sharing English lessons together at high school, I knew his writing style. To explain my knowing would be like trying to summarise how a poet can adeptly describe the seasons. It just is.

I glanced at Lorien, who still lay there in the same position, paying me no mind. I opened my mouth to accuse, and then thought better of it. Instead, I returned to the glow of the monitor and began to type my response.

Dear muzakman. How your beautiful words have charmed me. You have awoken the most desirous sensations within me, and although with another, I must act upon them.   Our destiny must not be ignored. It is as if an angel on high has brought us together and fate is now controlling the events about to unfold. We must meet, and soon. Until then, know that your DreamGoddess awaits our rendezvous with an anticipation never known.

I re-read it and it sounded corny. But hey, it was all part of the game wasn't it? A trickle of unease coursed through me after I had hit send. What if it *wasn't* Lorien?

I observed Lorien closely over the next few hours, sticking to him like gum on the proverbial shoe. When on the internet, I hovered around, feigning interest in some book, tidying the laptop nook surrounds, things like that. Not one opportunity did he get to have written the lengthy email I received the next morning. When had he found time to write this? He could have done it in longhand when scratching at his music notes, then typing it straight into an email. I stood, planning to seek out that notebook, then smiled, sitting again, to read the reply. I'd leave the sleuthing for later.

Oh fate, I thank you, and can't believe you have replied to me. Is it possible that my dreams may be realised? I imagine what our first kiss will be like, watching the sun set, the gentle breeze blowing to cool our heated bodies. And, with the sound of the waves crashing in time to the beating of my heart, I will take your hand in mine and listen to your heart match the rhythm of my own. I will take the warmth of your body into my arms and trace the softness of your skin, as I look into your eyes. You will smile at me and draw me closer to steal a kiss from you; a kiss I have been longing for. A kiss between two hearts falling in love, so special and to be shared by only we two. As our lips meet, my passion will soar to its zenith, dancing in the excitement of sharing that first kiss. I have longed for this moment, dreamt of it in so many scenarios, it is difficult to believe you will be here with me, together, alone.

Lorien was good at this. And I still had no doubt it *was* Lorien. I sure hoped so; otherwise, I was going to end up in a pile of... trouble! No mention had been made of meeting up, which surprised me. I would have thought that would be Lorien's 'step two' to this playacting. Unable to help myself, I went in search of him.

I finally found him stuffing the remnants of Christmas paper into the recycling bin. I sat on the front step watching him dump it in by the armful, pressing it down to make room for the empty glass bottles and cardboard boxes. When done, he flipped the lid down and brushed his hands together before placing them on his hips. A small nod of his head confirmed the mental ticking off on his 'things to do today before we leave for Mackay' list.

He turned and caught me smiling, his lips curling to match my own. He drew me upward to stand with him, the soulful kiss erasing the reason I had come in search of him, from my mind.

Standing there in the warmth of each other's embrace I again felt the flood of emotion as to how much I loved this man. This prompted me as to why I had come looking for him. I briefly struggled inwardly whether to mention it or not. I didn't want to spoil Lorien's game, and I *had* enjoyed the enticing and adventurous secret he had created. Life with Lorien was never going to be boring, that was for sure. No, I wouldn't mention anything, and I smiled up at him, leaning in for another kiss. However, he interrupted me before I had the chance. "Something?" he questioned, regarding my whimsical smile. It was as if he was just *daring* me to mention it.

"Nothing," I replied, leaning in to complete the interrupted kiss.

I drew away from him and looked down. I wanted that denim protrusion very badly, as obviously as he wanted to share it with me. Time was not our friend however, and he sighed, saying, "I know, packing to do!" I grinned at him and he ushered me back inside, his arm around my waist.

I looked around eagerly for Cara and Nick as we made our way up the walkway to the terminal, scanning the mass of happy faces awaiting their friends and relatives on our flight. Mercy was the first to spot them.

She launched herself at Nick who caught her neatly, swinging her around, making her legs fan out. "Poppy!" she exclaimed in the way that only the joy of a child can express. She kissed him hard on the lips with a big *mwuah* sound and he hugged her to him. We three had said our hellos to Cara during this heart-warming scene, then swapped. Nick passed Mercy to Cara and she repeated her award-winning performance.

Lorien then took Mercy in his arms, as much as her squiggling around tried to fight it, and we headed to the baggage claim. We were taking no chance of losing Mercy in this sea of exultant human holiday traffic.

The house smelled and looked wonderful. Cara had always excelled with decorating, and now she had the antique shop, the house was furnished with quaint collections of yore. The twins and I set the table, chatting all the while to their parents as they tackled the tasks in the kitchen. Mercy sat perched at a kitchen stool talking above us in her sing-song storytelling way, enlightening Nanny and Poppy of the excitement her life had become since turning three. Luckily, they both had two ears.

Déjà vu all over again... Here I sat, stuffed, adorning a silly hat and toying with my pudding, having no intention of eating any more. Mercy was excused to play with her new stash as we all helped clear the table. Nick then took the twins outside to show them his new shed, complete with pool and foosball tables, and Cara and I headed for the lounge to drink our coffees. "So, what did Lorien get you for Christmas Ashlyn?" she asked.

"I don't know yet," I answered in all honesty. "He has been driving me crazy for weeks now, and you know how short my patience is!" Cara laughed with me, and I searched her face for any sign of knowing. She was not as easy to read as Lorien, but it appeared Cara was none-the-wiser either.

Around eight o'clock, I marvelled at how peaceful the house had become. Cara had headed upstairs about half an hour ago, and the rest of the Standish men were asleep, sprawled out either on the lawn under the shade of the gigantic Leichhardt tree, namely the twins, or in the hammock tethered likewise to its trunk, Nick, with Mercy lying face down over his chest, also asleep. The mild, warm breeze cast a gentle, soothing sway to the hammock's inhabitants, keeping them in their 'rock-a-bye baby' doze.

I don't know what I had done in a previous life, but it was obviously something wonderful for me to have achieved such bliss.

Mercy started to stir, shifting slightly in Nick's large embrace. She looked so tiny held within his arms, so fragile and elfin. Her head rolled, leaving her face-to-armpit with her beloved Poppy. The soft hair tickled at her nose, and so she rolled back again, her nose crinkling with an incessant itch. My smile conveyed the joy I took from this simple, yet loving scene.

I cast my glance toward Elijah, strong, dutiful Elijah. Thinking back to our 'glory days' of dating, I briefly wondered how we Standish's had actually evolved into the relationship we all had within the family realms. How different would my life have been if things hadn't changed? Would Elijah and I still have been a couple all these years later? Would children have ensued? Although an impossible question to answer, it was a valid one.

And finally, I looked to my darling Lorien - shirtless, bronzed, lying on his back with his hands tucked behind his head. He slept the sleep of the innocent, the brave, the true. His love for me, and likewise, mine for him, was something musicians wrote of, including Lorien. Was every person destined to find this kind of unfathomable love? Or, was I the lucky one, not having to traverse the universe in search of my soul mate?

I let my eyes trickle down over his rippled stomach, narrow waist and lean, long legs. There was nothing I didn't find sexy about this man, and oh dear God, there was never a time I didn't want to act on it. Lorien was simply delicious!

As his eyes flitted slowly open, they came to rest on my own, twinkling back at him, smiling in our secret way. A smile could say it all. He beckoned me over to him with one gesturing finger and I moved silently across the lawn, laying my head across his broad chest.

The light summer breeze fingered through my hair, matching the movement of his caress. I leant up and kissed him, loving the tranquillity, the scent of the day, the soft yielding grass beneath us. How I would love to lay like this forever, in the arms of my handsome Prince, my Knight in shining armour. However, I was content to hold this moment and closed my eyes to savour it. I too at some stage dozed off.

It was when the gentle night breeze started to whirl and eddy the Leichhardt tree's refuse around the yard, I woke, still bundled within Lorien's clinch. "Big storm coming!" Cara called from the top step, her skirt snapping briskly at her legs. She turkey-trotted down the stairs to help Mercy climb off Nick. A hammock containing two on a blustery evening is not easy to escape from unaided. Mercy's eyes were huge as Cara carried her back into the house.

Nick and the twins set about securing loose items around the yard and I picked up all the things we'd brought out over the course of the afternoon. As we finally shut the screen door behind us, the night exploded in a cacophony of noise and radiance. The lightning zippered open the sky seconds before the timpani drum of the thunder boomed.

We sat watching the acoustic lightshow from the front verandah, feasting on the leftovers of either turkey or ham sandwiches. A resounding flash followed by a sonic crack left the air thick with the scent of ozone. Cara glanced nervously at Mercy before giving Lorien a silent mother's look, letting him know she was taking her inside. I think Cara had had enough of the torment as well.

Not that many hours later, I crawled into bed as Lorien threw the curtains wide, leaving our view of the still raging storm unobstructed. As he moved in beside me, I curled in under his arm, running my fingers lightly across his smooth chest. Trance-like, we lay like that until a new brilliance converted the dark sky into day again. I waited on the duet reply of the thunder and jumped when it finally announced itself. "It's heading away," Lorien said, noting the timing between the lightning and the thunder was increasing.

"I love the rain," I murmured in response.

"I love you," he answered, his hand moving down to cup my breast, a curious finger teasing over my nipple. I smiled up at him, wanting his kiss. My lips parted to him, a searching tongue finding my own. And as the ebbing flickers of turbulence continued to silently flash, we indulged in each other, emulating the force of the departing storm.

Mackay

"But I can't get by on my own.
I need my family,
How it's grown."

L Standish, 'Relative Relatives'

MY CHRISTMAS SURPRISE from Lorien announced itself a few days later. I was out of patience; only knowing it was coming, not knowing what it could possibly be. It was over breakfast this morning that Lorien looked at me with a grin. "Today's the day," he announced. The rest of the family kept eating, ignoring him, yet with knowing smiles on each of their faces. All faces, other than Mercy's.

"What are we doing today Orrie?" she asked, thinking it was always about her. A sideways glance from Lorien made her correct herself. "Daddy."

You are going to be staying with your grandparents for a few days. Your mother and I are taking off on our own little holiday. He had my undivided attention.

"Where?" I asked.

"KoHuna Sands Resort, where the rainforest meets the reef," he announced with a grandiose flare of his hands - jazz hands. I laughed.

"You will love it Ashlyn," Cara offered. "Nick and I spent a week there when we first moved up here. They have everything; and as for the area, what isn't at the Resort is only a short distance from it. The Whitsundays, Barrier Reef, Brampton Island, beaches, rainforest – the list is endless."

"In fact, I'd say it was a perfect secluded spot for a second honeymoon," Nick added, smiling at me.

"Go Mum and Dad," Elijah chirped in. Cara swatted his arm with her napkin.

"Elijah!" she reprimanded. Nick laughed and stood, kissing Cara on the top of her head before clearing away the breakfast dishes.

"So, what am I doing?" Mercy complained. She obviously wanted to come with us.

"You, Poppy and I are going to have our own fun!" Cara said. Mercy brightened a little at this.

"And Unkie Lie?"

"I have to be getting home Sweetie. It's time for me to get back to work."

It was a shame Elijah had to leave earlier than the rest of us. At times, it was to his detriment that his schedule was not as easy-going as Lorien's, and that Mercy and I were at the 'mercy' of the NSW state government. When I was on holidays, so was Mercy, and therefore so was Lorien. It was a perfect situation really, although it was going to be wonderful to spend some time alone with each other. An hour later, we were on our way.

The bungalow we were staying in had all the trimmings; a queen bed, kitchen, lounge and private courtyard. I had a fair idea of Lorien's plans for that courtyard! I certainly hoped so. He would prove me wrong however by adding another far more sinister location to his list.

In all innocence, I climbed into the car, eager to see where we were going. After a thirty-kilometre drive south, we pulled into a carpark and Lorien switched off the engine. "I thought we might start with a view of the local surrounds." I smiled and nodded, allowing him to assist me from the car. Lorien was still the perfect gentleman he'd always been.

The view from the top of the lookout was breathtaking. The busy port below us hummed and vibrated with the noise and activity of the coal trains and ship loaders. The bulk carriers sat waiting on the horizon, but whether drawing closer or leaving the area with full cargo, was unknown from this distance.

As we circled the top of the lookout, Lorien glanced toward me. "'S'cuse me," he pardoned himself as he worked through the gaps within the few people sharing our space, to manoeuvre me to the rear of the platform.

"What?" I started. He placed a finger to my lips softly; his eyes did not contain the same soothing gesture... nor did his hands. He pinched my rear once, then flitted under my skirt, tugging at the rim of my briefs. "*No!*" I hissed at him, trying not to laugh. An elderly man directly in front of me turned sideways and Lorien relaxed back into his pose, making it seem nothing untoward was going on. I however stiffened like a pole. This then enabled him to pull my briefs straight down my legs unheeded, as soon as the man faced back toward the beautiful scenery before us.

"I will rip them off you if you don't raise your feet," he threatened quietly. I raised first one foot, then the other, allowing him access. Lorien then balled up my briefs, shoving them into his pocket. I moved to the other side of the platform, bumping into the now retreating man, and away from the lecherous grin encasing Lorien's face. He twitched one eyebrow at me, letting me know escape was not that easy.

The only other people, a family of four, left soon after, leaving us alone. Lorien crossed the small space in under a second and had me

against the edge. I pushed him off me. "No Lorien, and besides, it hurts."
I gestured toward the round metal handrail fixed to the three enclosed
fenced walls of the platform, which had been digging into my back.

"Sorry," he said and pulled me toward him. I was then hoisted
onto the railing; Lorien nestled between my splayed thighs.

"Lorien," I whispered, so very scared of being caught and as if by
summons, the stairs clattered, signalling yet another arrival.

Still fully clothed, Lorien thought this delicious. He, however, was
not the one with spread legs and no underwear on, with a man wedged up
against him, concrete in response. To sweeten the scenario for the
newcomers, he circled my shoulders with his arms and kissed lightly at my
cheek, portraying the innocent young lovers we no longer were. The
couple in their mid-forties smiled at me sweetly and turned their backs,
leaving us to it. And how did I know this? I never took my eyes off them
the entire time.

They left in less than ten minutes, but during this time, Lorien had
eased up my skirt and had been slowly pressing and rubbing himself
against me. The coarse denim of his jeans had been working electrically
against the most sensitive areas of my private self. It was all I could do to
repress my groans and maintain a level of composure. I smiled cheekily
at him when he brought one hand down toward me, thinking he was going
to massage me a little, manually. But the whisper of his zip told me
another story. As his hardness forced into my softness I gasped, knowing
there was nothing I could do to stop this now. We were making love, in
public!

I lay back as far as the mesh fencing would permit, allowing
Lorien a better angle, of which he took full advantage. He ran his thumb
briefly over my drawn lips, my teeth biting into them to hide the gasps that

wanted to be heard. He drew my bottom lip down with that thumb, easing it inside my mouth. Now moistened, he lowered it to press against me, circling gently.

The previous teeth-biting containment vanished, and I let my moans verbally portray the building that was surging inside me. Lorien then froze, and I looked up at him in disappointment before he drew my cheek to his chest, his arms folding me to him. In that sideways glance, I could see two heads bobbing up the stairs. I was glad Lorien had been paying attention, as I was in another world.

As he drew my face slowly back, he smiled knowingly down at me, now sharing the unexpected interlude with me. He chuckled darkly, forcing himself into me just that little bit further. To suppress my groan, he kissed me, dancing his tongue over my own, duplicating what his thumb had been so beautifully doing, albeit further south.

Again, our stance left nothing uncovered, but the newcomers were not idiots. I heard a muted intake of breath and then an audible, "Oh!" They were gone seconds later, soft sniggering ebbed away with their retreat. We laughed, but only for a moment, as Lorien re-engaged the heat and thrust into me once again.

The chain mail of the fence tinkled its melodic tune in time with our own growing crescendo, and I reached my arms up to lace my fingers through it, stabilising me. Lorien quickly unbuttoned my shirt, and shoved my bra up, allowing him to watch his force jiggle my breasts in time to his movement. He did not watch for long though, leaning in to suckle me, never losing his stride.

He groaned again, and this time pulled out from me completely, grabbing me from the rail and spinning me around so my back was against him. I looked quickly over my shoulder to see how many had arrived this time, and was surprised to see no one standing there.

A hand on my left knee guided it onto the rail as he grasped my hip with his other hand. He rucked my skirt halfway up my back and entered me, my fingers again searching out the harsh metal diamonds for support.

Overlooking the magnificent scene, the glint of sun-sparkle splashed over distant objects, setting the view on fire. As my orgasm flashed, I lowered my forehead to the mesh fencing, making Lorien drive harder and further into me, becoming rigid within me instantly. His hands slid up my arms slowly, then retreated, coming to lay on my breasts again which he caressed, my nipples still stiff between his supple fingers. His coarse breath found the sweet spot on my nape and he kissed lightly there, before turning me again to face him. "I love you so much Ash," he crooned before leaning in to kiss me. And this time my fingers sought out his silky curls, holding him to me. I loved him just as much.

Our timing had been perfect. Minutes later a tour bus of people climbed to the lookout. Lorien still held me in his arms, and I found myself trance-like, listening to the slowing boom of his heartbeat. It was only the trickle of his pearl trail creeping down my inner thigh that made me draw back, my mouth a silent circle of surprise, my eyes wide. He laughed loudly, aware of what my face was betraying, making the sightseers glance toward us, wondering what joke they had missed. He hugged me to him, running his hand over my back soothingly, as I clamped my knees together. "Come on, let's go," he whispered, and I trotted, stiff legged, through the crowd and down the stairs, with Lorien's soft laughter ushering me.

"That was NOT funny!" I reprimanded as we walked through the bush trails shortly after, hand in hand. His chuckle begged to differ and chose not to answer my school-marm attitude. "Can I have my undies back now," I asked, and he smiled at me, slowly shaking his head. He was infectious, and I smiled back.

We glanced at the signage posted around the track, outlining a rare tree or bush. Neither of us was enthused nature buffs, but still wanted to embrace the flora that surrounded us, taking full advantage of the new environment. As Lorien went to step off the track, my hand went to his shoulder, stopping him. "Where are you going?" I whispered, although I don't know why I felt that was necessary. There wasn't a soul in sight.

"I just spotted something and want a closer look, come on," he urged.

"But we're not supposed to go off the trail," I argued.

"Says who?" was his response before leading me through the slight brush barrier into the depth of the rainforest.

A few metres in, I could feel the cool envelope me. The dappled sunlight played through in only a few places, and the echoing call of the various birds was a symphony of woodwinds, the insects and cicadas providing the strings. The soft, mossy expanse in front of us was Lorien's destination, and that was where we stopped. He stripped off his shirt and shorts, laying them blanket-like on the ground. "Why do you still have your joggers on?" I asked, most curious of his answer, considering the comical sight before me. His simple response made me shudder,

"Leeches." I looked around in vain; there was no way I'd know I had picked one up until it started to suck my blood and make me itch. I then sat, centre-square on his clothes, to avoid the little vampires.

"Why do you have your clothes *off*?" I asked with a laugh. It was a stupid question. He straddled himself over one of my legs, and kissed me, forcing me back to lie on the cushioned layer beneath me. Working the knee centred between mine, it climbed higher up my thighs, in search of the warmth of my junction. When it reached the destination, it was then I who was straddling him. I parted for him, still slick with desire. He kissed me, then drew back, lowering himself down to explore the territory more thoroughly that he had awoken.

His hands were a silk caress as they lowered my knees outward, moving himself forward so all that was visible to me were his eyes peering over my rise. The small crinkle in them then portrayed the smile I could not see. Lightly pinching my lower folds together, the flesh surrounding my jewel opened fanlike before him, leaving me vulnerable to his ministrations. He circled his tongue above, beneath and around, never quite hitting the target, building me slowly, tormentingly. The gentle pinch continued, one finger gliding through to separate me every so often, just to remind me of its presence.

As my breaths became shallow gasps, Lorien stopped, saying, "Finish this off on top of me Baby." We quickly repositioned, and I impaled myself over him, putting me back in control. I leant back and closed my eyes, savouring the sounds and scents that surrounded us, feeling so alive and tranquil; in perfect balance. Lorien's hands found my hips again, rocking me in a dual rhythm.

For the second time within the hour, I reached the high plains. As I slowed the tempo, I looked down into Lorien's soulful eyes. He reached up and brushed the hair from my forehead, whispering, "I love you."

I lay in his arms until the coolness of the canopied womb crept in. Neither of us wanted to leave this hidden paradise, but it's not as if we couldn't come back.

Our next interlude was more innocent than the last and included actual sightseeing. I felt like an absolute knob as I waddled onto the glass-bottomed boat, completely decked out in navy coloured scuba gear. "Flick and slap," Lorien instructed showing me how to walk in flippers, but I was not known for my athletic ability, unlike some twins I knew. He made it look easy, and he also looked very hot in his matching scuba gear, but in red.

Once we had taken a seat on the bench that surrounded the inside circumference of the 'aft' side of the boat, Lorien kicked his flippers off, setting them under the bench beneath him. He turned to me and grinned. "You son of a ..." he cut me off mid-sentence.

"Please don't refer to my mother in that way," he said and laughed, hugging me to him.

"We didn't need to have them on?" I asked, miffed.

"No."

"So, you told me to put them on for your amusement?"

"Yes." This time I had to laugh with him. I was certainly not naive, but at times quite gullible. I rolled my eyes at him and sighed. I should have been used to it by now.

When the boat was full, we set sail. Well, started the engines to be more exact, and headed to sea. I peered eagerly through the glass-bottom panel in the centre of the seating, waiting to catch a glimpse of something, anything. I wasn't as keen as Lorien to go snorkelling, having seen 'Jaws' one too many times, but I was prepared to give it a go. I had not seen even a minute minnow through the glass window, so felt safer knowing there was little life around. "They'll start feeding in a sec," Lorien told me, catching the look on my face, thinking it disappointment at the lack of aquatic life. He was wrong.

"Oh?"

"Yes, and then you'll see some action. The fish around here are used to these charters and tend to follow the boats once fed. It makes for a better experience when you're guaranteed of some sights."

"Oh," I responded, with less enthusiasm.

Sure enough, a few massive angelfish swam into view below us, and then the waters turned into rush-hour traffic. A turtle darted past at one point, and a slow, lumbering fish I didn't recognise, mouth agape, seconds later. Other than that, the rest were fish whipping in and out of my vision, faster than my gaze could comprehend. And then the motors slowed, then stopped. "Time for a swim," Lorien said, pulling on his flippers, and adjusting his mask.

He stood and put his hand out to assist me to my feet. My feet had other ideas. "Ahhh, I don't know Lorien."

"Just give it a try Ash, even for a few minutes." His hand never wavered, still waiting on me to take it and stand.

I glanced over the edge of the boat, and seeing nothing, checked the glass panel in the floor for further visual information. The action had slowed measurably and now only an odd fish swam past. "If the fish were eating, then surely that brings in bigger fish to feed on them?" I reasoned with him.

"The waters are too warm here for 'Jaws'," he answered with a laugh, picking up on my unspoken point. I trusted him, and I took his hand and stood with him, waiting on our turn to enter the water.

I listened carefully to the dive instructor as I adjusted my own mask and snorkel, before descending the short ladder into the sea. "Don't leave us behind like in 'Open Water'," I said around the snorkel mouthpiece. He and Lorien shared a laugh and Lorien said,

"She watches too much TV." I shot him a dirty look, and finally let go of the ladder. At that very moment, one of those huge angelfish came within a metre of me, and I reversed my movement, reaching for the ladder and shoving a now-descending Lorien back up.

"Up! Lorien, get out of my way!" I screamed at him. I was now in full panic, and I was the cause of it. A few of the other swimmers looked nervously around, not sure what had scared me. One or two ducked their heads under the water to see what may be lurking. Of course, there was nothing dangerous circling just out of the light, nor raging at them from the murky depths.

I collapsed on the deck, once Lorien and the instructor pulled me up the ladder, whooping in lungfuls of air as I laugh-cried. I knew how stupid I had been, but was still fighting the adrenalin rush from my fright. Lorien was not laughing. "What was it Ash? What scared you?" His concern made me giggle, now more composed and breathing more regularly again.

"A fish."

"Just a fish? Not a shark?"

"No, just a fish." Seeing everything was now OK, the instructor continued to assist the other sightseers, and letting people know everything was OK.

"You goose," Lorien said and smiled, cupping my chin in his hand, lowering his lips to my nose for a quick peck.

"I know, right," I said and laughed. Lorien helped me to my feet, and I took the stupid flippers off, taking a seat. "I'll be right here when you get back," I told him, patting the bench. Lorien grinned, and I watched until he disappeared down the ladder, out of sight.

New Year's Eve was upon us, which signalled our little holiday within our holiday, about to end. We had tomorrow at the bungalow, which I assumed would be spent nursing a 'welcome to day one of the new year' hangover, before we were to head back to Mackay, and then the next day, home. We had decided to coop ourselves up in the room for the night, plenty of champagne and room service at our disposal; the 9 pm and midnight fireworks easily viewed from our courtyard.

Lorien had been busy for an hour writing little notes and dropping them into one of the two coffee mugs in front of him. I finally put an end to it by pouring some champagne and putting the music system on the table outside. "Come on Lover, you've been at that long enough," I prompted, running my hand slowly across his shoulders, trying to peer past him to catch a glimpse of what he had been up to. He jumped slightly at my touch, then turned and smiled up at me.

"Wow, I was miles away," he admitted, then pulled me down onto his lap. Tucking my hair behind my ears, his hands then formed to the sides of my throat, drawing me in for a kiss. "Another end to a wonderful year," he whispered, nuzzling at my ear, his breath a maddening electrifying switch.

"Yes Sweetheart, always," I replied. "Come on, let's enjoy the rest of what's left of the afternoon," I said, standing, and dragging him to his feet to follow me outside. I didn't get very far, as Lorien reached backward and grabbed the two paper-filled mugs.

Seated outside, he finally put an end to the writing mystery. "Pick one from each," he instructed. So I did. In my left hand I had a solitary word written 'fondle' and in my right, again one solitary word, 'boobs'. I got the gist of the game immediately and shook my head, returning the papers to their respective mugs.

"Nuh uh, Lorien," I reprimanded. "This is going to end up being a sex-fest for you!"

"And you Baby," he reminded, pushing the mugs toward me again for a second pluck.

"One mug is full of verbs and the other, of nouns?" I asked. His nod confirmed this. "Nuh, uh," I reiterated.

"Well, you write either the verbs or nouns then," he said, holding the mugs in front of me to select one of the options.

"Can I do both?" I asked and laughed, knowing he was not going to allow this. He didn't, so I chose the nouns. And it was a wise choice.

I sat, considering what to write, as Lorien tore fresh paper for me. When I was done, I placed them all into the now empty noun mug and smiled at him, ready for the game.

He drew first. He squidged his chair over closer to mine and took my hand, raising my elbow to his mouth. He laughed, then sucked on my elbow for a few seconds, making a face at me. "Are they all going to be like this Ash?" he asked when finished with my elbow. I grinned at him with a smart-arsed look on my face.

"Yep!" Knowing the game was now over, I reached for the mugs, tipping out the verbs. I knew what was in the noun mug. I knew it! Suck, fondle, rub, stroke, lick... You name it; any deviant type of behaviour was accounted for. Lorien wrinkled his nose at me and smiled when I glanced up at him.

"Thought I would give it a shot," he said, shrugging his shoulders in innocence. I climbed onto his lap, circling him in my embrace.

"Honey, you don't need to play these games with me to be near me, be with me," I said.

"I know, but I thought it would be fun."

"Without the usual crowd of jeering fools," I said and laughed.

"I'm not Michael," he said. No, he was not. As I reflected over this, I felt his hand creep up under my shirt, finding my breast. "I never got to do the first one you picked," he admitted, sealing his mouth to mine, keeping his hand busy. I didn't mind.

We weren't in too poor of a state New Year's Day. I did not want to get out of bed though when Lorien started to stir at 7 am. I rolled back over and yanked the covers above my head, shepherding my intention to be left for a while longer. And amazingly, he did.

Some unknown time later, I was roused from my slight doze by the weightlessness of the covers no longer on me, and the morning sparkle of sunshine dancing across my squinty face. "Lor-ee-en!" I complained, trying to turn away from the light, but he had drawn all the curtains and there was no refuge for my searching face. So, I opened my eyes and readied myself for the new day. The new year! And what a year it was going to be.

Lorien already had room service deliver breakfast, and I was famished. The snacks from last night were no alternative for a proper sized meal. He sipped on his coffee as he watched me ladle out various breakfast foods onto two plates. I finished by planting a kiss to the tip of his nose. "There", I said in a breathy tone, taking a seat, ready to feast. It was all so good.

And finally, it was check-out time. That was OK though, as we still had tonight with Lorien's parents, and I was also missing our home.

Whilst packing our bags, Lorien addressed the New Year's Eve resolutions we had failed to make the night before. "Can I make yours?" I asked.

"Only if I can make yours," Lorien said, raising his eyebrows. I agreed.

I had been thinking about what to make for Lorien right through our check-out, and now we were on our way back to Mackay, decided they were a pretty sad and uneventful list of nothing. "Have you made my resolution for me yet?" I asked, bringing us back down the conversation path again.

"Yep. Ready?" I nodded, yes. "You have to promise to love and care for me, for the rest of my life, considering no other, until the day I die."

"Oh Lorien," I cried, hugging him to me. "Of course, my Darling, and well beyond that! That will also be my resolution for you." He kissed me, sealing our agreement, the same agreement we had made on our wedding day, and even before. The romantic in him never ceased to amaze me, and I was so thankful of his loving nature. Both of us knowing this resolution was already in place, did not remove the wonder of having him reconfirm it to me again and again and again. I loved him so much. And the resolution I made to him was definitely not going to be difficult to maintain.

On our return to the parental home at Mackay all was quiet and no one seemed to be home. It was then that we realised we had no key to let ourselves in. We dragged our luggage onto the front verandah, and headed for the cooler, breezy backyard and the shade of the Leichhardt tree. Lorien climbed into the hammock and beckoned for me to join him. Getting one into a hammock was a trial, but adding a second person was a nightmare. I managed to end up in his immediate embrace, scrambling into the netting with the grace of an ostrich on water-skis. Sharing a hammock certainly made good friends of you!

Once settled against each other, with me in Lorien's arms, the gentle sway of the hammock spread its hypnotic effect and we rocked with it, lying in silence, dreaming of yesterdays and tomorrows.

Mercy's mad dash from the front of the house to the backyard broke our reverie, bringing us back to today. My eyes had been closed, but I was not asleep. I let Mercy think that I was… we were… as Lorien did not move either. "Up, up, up!" she chanted, and her hot, squirmy little body was upon us, adding a third person to the fray. I copped a knee to my breast, and Lorien to the underside of his chin, as she rearranged herself.

Nick was standing by the hammock, the unseen lifter, and started to swing it from side to side, much stronger than our gentle lull had been. "Yay!" Mercy called, encouraging him, before turning her attention to us. She covered our faces with little kisses, and hugged us fiercely, one after the other. We had only been gone a short while, but a greeting like this on our return was magical. We were such a loving family, and our girl had been raised with the same affection.

"I missed you Mummy, I missed you Orrie!" she chirped, hugging us again. At least she was getting better with the 'Mummy' title.

"We missed you too Bump!" I confirmed, and ran a finger down her little calf, brown as a berry."

"You *have* been using sun-screen on her, haven't you Dad?" Lorien asked Nick, also noticing her rich colouring.

"No, son," Nick answered in good-humoured sarcasm. "This is the first kid I've ever been in contact with!" Lorien really shouldn't have been surprised as to her tan; she got it from him.

Over dinner Mercy gave us a complete run-down of her activities during our absence. Nick and Cara had taken her to every theme park in Queensland, it seemed, which certainly explained her healthy bronzed little body. Today's quest had been 'White Water World'. "Such a shame Mercy doesn't have a brother or sister yet," Cara said. "You should have seen Nick on the rides with her over the past few days." She delivered this line with a smirk. Lorien and I caught her meaning at the same time, and burst out laughing at the thought of Nick on little rides. Mercy was not the kind of child to sit and wave at you as she went by. We were well aware of this. Poor Nick.

Nick and Cara dropped us at the airport the next day, our goodbyes taken care of at the front of the entry doors. Our flight was departing in half an hour so seemed silly for them to waste money on parking fees.

After we checked in, I took a seat whilst Lorien took Mercy up to the huge glass windows overlooking the tarmac. Together they watched the hubbub of the metropolis outside.

I took this opportunity to write one last email to *muzakman*, ending our promise of any future together. I assumed Lorien would find this funny, and also sweet, considering our mutual new year resolutions we made for each other.

Dear muzakman. Alas, it is with a saddened heart that I must end our dalliance, for it can never evolve. I have found myself even deeper in love with my current soul mate that the thought of being with another, I simply cannot comprehend. I hope you find your life-love and spend the rest of your days as happy as I know I will be. DreamGoddess. Not Shakespeare, but good enough. I smiled and looked up, and Lorien stood before me with Mercy in his arms.

"What are you up to Mummy?" he asked with a glint in his eye. I fully suspected that he would be aware of what I had been up to, not very long from now.

"Nothing Sweetheart!" I chirped and closed my iPhone. "Shall we use the bathroom before we board?" I asked, taking Mercy from him. He just shook his head and smiled, and we headed to the toilets, hand in hand.

I took little notice of Lorien flicking through his phone during the flight. Not until he put the screen in front of me, showing me my reply to Muzakman. "I knew it was you all along," I said, raising one eyebrow, and snuggling in under the arm he had raised, making room for me.

"Did you now?" he replied, amused. I looked up at him and nodded. "And what if it hadn't been? Hmmmm?" he questioned.

"I suppose after we had arranged to meet, at least halfway through the sex I would have realised it wasn't you and been one hell of a surprised lady!"

"Oh Ashlyn," he laughed lowly, pressing my brow against his chest. His fingers worked into my hair, stroking lightly as I heard him sigh, "My Ashlyn, my dream goddess..." I closed my eyes, a smile playing to my lips as I felt his on my temple.

THREE...

Casual Full Time

"I want to be beside you, crawl inside you,
Won't you let me in?
I have to have you, merge and fuse you,
And be my natural twin."

L Standish, 'Doppelganger'

ANNUAL SCHOOL SPORT DAY! Yay! Something I dreaded whilst attending school had come to bite me again in adult life. When in Year 7 and not knowing how things worked, I did participate in the cross-country, swimming and athletics trials. However, by Year 8, I was wise to the situation, and had a note for each and every one, each and every year.

The history of the sport teams name choices was hilarious when looking at their background. I myself was in Simpson house when at school and had no idea of who he was or why he was relevant to Sommersett. And, our historical local celebrities consisted of: Captain William Reid - who became the first European to make his way into Lake Macquarie, attributed to a shocking sense of direction; Lieutenant Percy Simpson – who constructed the Great North Road between Sydney and Castlebrook, settling in Warden; Moses Carroll – one of Simpson's convicts who took over the Simpson Warden property as a stockman and later became the constable of the area; and Lieutenant Jonathon Warner - Simpson's predecessor and an army officer employed as a surveyor on the Great North Road until he was replaced due to his shoddy work. Yes, these people were part of our area's heritage. No, they were not the greatest of folk heroes to be naming the school's four sport houses after. I had to agree with the students, it was time to update the system.

However, it was not my decision to make, although I had made mention of it to the Headmistress, Mrs Lawper. I had gained from my conversation, the job of updating the school song. I needed to learn to keep my mouth shut!

Poor Simpson and Carroll houses were always vying to *not* take last place at the carnivals – any of the carnivals, whether athletics, cross country or swimming. Reid and Warner were therefore always vying for first place. Nothing had changed over the years between leaving school and returning as a teacher, and again, I was assigned to Simpson house as a staff member.

I was fortunate in one way when I was a student in Simpson. Some of my best friends at the time, namely, Frankie, Cyndi, Keren, Simon and Bree were all in Simpson house as well. Michael was in Warner and was constantly being chased from Simpson's seating area by the teachers, all day. His blue shirt stood out fabulously against our red ones. It became quite the game of cat and mouse for him. Even when the Standish's came to town, nothing changed. They were both assigned to Reid and were sporty, so their day took on a whole different focus to the rest of us. Even Simon and Michael took on the odd event.

Part of my role now as a teacher in Simpson was to become *that* bitch teacher, who chased students back to their own areas, and made the non-participants cheer all day for Simpson house. Blechh. I was more likely to sit with the Simpson music students, who were often non-participants. Being artistic certainly did not mean you weren't also athletic, but it wasn't often I saw these two worlds collide. Unless you were born a Standish...

I used this common factor of musical versus athletic students to keep me out of the firing line as well. At times, I offered shelter to a Reid, Carroll, or Warner music student, who had joined our group. The school musical was about to go into pre-production and those interested were excited and eager to discuss it. When you were a music student by choice, you were expected to be in the band, choir, or as a cast member. Otherwise, why were you in my classes?

Just after lunch, Mrs Lawper strolled past, interrupting our little musical group. "Busy planning with the students Mrs Standish?" she asked in genuine involvement.

"Yes Mrs Lawper, we certainly are!" I answered, sending a smile around to the group seated with me. They respectfully smiled back, nodding, showing their excitement for music to be *way* more appealing than sport.

"And how is the new version of the school song progressing?" Mrs Lawper asked.

"Fine, it's finished."

"Excellent, I would love to hear it tomorrow if you can fit me into your music period. When would suit?" *Shit! Shit, shit, shit!* It was not finished! I had not even *started* it yet. My big mouth once again had put me in peril.

"Any period after lunch would be fine," I answered, smiling.

"Wonderful, see you then," she said, and continued on her way.

"Excuse me kids, I have to check on something," I offered lamely to the students sitting with me. "Best you non-Simpsonites head back to your own houses for now," I said, ushering them off. I then headed straight home, hoping my absence wouldn't be noticed.

Lorien met me at the door. He must have seen my mad dash across the road from the school. His response was what I expected as he flung open the door. "Oh Baby! Some afternoon delight!" He was standing there, full-blown erection, without a stitch of clothing on. I was hoping Mercy was down for a nap!

"No!" I called, pushing him from me. But he thought this was all part of the playful foreplay and continued to wrangle with me. "No Lorien!" I said again, pushing him with more force. His face fell. "Oh Honey, I am sorry, but I have a massive problem and I need your help." His face softened when he heard the angst in my voice and the mirrored, worried look on my face.

"What's happened?" he asked, concern now creeping into his own. I started to babble, getting out the key words only in my random, chaotic prattle. "OK, calm down," he said, leading me to the bathroom where he swathed a towel around his naked hips. I took a few breaths and smiled up at him. He kissed me on the nose and led me into the kitchen, putting on the kettle for a cup of tea.

Over the soothing hot liquid, I managed to get the story out, and in a less garbled way. "Well, that's no problem, I can have it for you by morning," he confirmed.

"I will be stealing your work Lorien. I don't feel very proud of myself for getting into this mess, and I am so sorry you will have to give me the credit for something you've written." He smiled at me kindly.

"For better or for worse remember?" This was certainly not one of the betters.

"And there's one thing more…" I continued. He raised one eyebrow, waiting on me to continue. "I need it tonight. I have to have time to practice it." I looked down, feeling like the worst crud that gets caught in a shoe tread. How could I be doing this to him?

"No problem," he again confirmed. I launched myself at him and covered his face with kisses. My world, my rock! My Lorien. How I did love him. I was slightly suspicious that he felt the same way about me. "So... the afternoon delight?" How could I refuse, but I had to.

"I am still on duty, Mr Standish!" I said, now standing in front of him. He clapped his hands to his lap, beckoning me back. I shook my head. He clapped his lap. "Lorien, you have a piece of music to write for me. And some lyrics too!"

"Lyrics too! Sweet Jesus Ashlyn. Let's hope Merce stays asleep a bit longer hey! This may take a while." Great, I now felt guilty again, and that I hadn't even checked on my girl whilst home. But, I simply sighed, kissed him goodbye and headed back to school.

On my arrival home a couple of hours later, I found the sheet music sitting on the dining room table. I headed toward the piano, mentally playing the notes in my head, trying to familiarise them as quickly as possible. Oh My God! What had he done? Lorien had not created a few chorded, little school ditty; he had composed a symphony. Or, more aptly put for me, a requiem. This would be the death of me! The intricate trills and many-faceted orchestra parts, key changes and even aria choir parts caused me to flump onto the piano stool, deflated. And then I started to laugh. My Lorien. How had he managed to get this done in the time I'd left the house? "Something funny?" I heard behind me.

"Hi Baby!" Mercy cried, and Lorien passed her to me from his hip.

"Mummy," I corrected out of habit, but this time in a robotic drone as Lorien still had my full attention. Mercy did not respond, but started to plink out a nothing tune on the piano, sitting on my lap.

"She takes after us," Lorien said, and sat next to me, taking my hand. He then leant in for a kiss.

"Of course she does Honey," I answered, looking up at him softly, tucking a curl behind his ear. I started to snicker again.

"What? Don't you like it?" he asked, brow furrowed. I had never been able to offer him any criticism, as there was none to offer, so my reaction had caused some concern in him.

"Honey, this is supposed to be a replacement for the current, massively outdated, school anthem. You have given me a composition, not a simple song."

"And I believe it *is* time for a rehaul. School songs, anthems, whatever you want to call them, are becoming too jingle-like and it's time to return them to the propriety for which they stand."

"Wow," was my response. "I had no idea you felt that way."

"Damn right! And the same goes for National Anthems as well."

"Damn right!" Mercy parroted. I shot Lorien a look, and he laughed. We chose to ignore her though. I wondered whether she did it deliberately, wanting the attention she knew she got when using wrong or bad language. I didn't have time to contemplate the point now though.

"Anyway," Lorien continued, "this is the result, and this is how I feel about it. I went to that school too remember, and I wanted to represent how I felt, we all felt, about attending there. It's where we fell in love."

"I know," I said, hugging him to me. "I just hope I can pull it off. *And*, that Mrs Lawper doesn't suspect who the composer was. She may find it too elaborate as well. But, if she does, it will buy me some more time to complete it myself."

Straight after lunch the next day, Mrs Lawper knocked at the music room door. My students looked up, not expecting to see the Headmistress standing there, and were suitably curious as to her arrival. Mrs Lawper took a seat at the rear of the room, smiled and nodded. Knowing there was little else I could do, I stood and addressed the class. "Mrs Lawper has joined us today, *briefly*," I added, hoping I had not stressed the word too greatly, "to hear the new version of the school song I have written." I nearly swallowed the word 'I', knowing it was a big, fat lie. With that, I sat at the piano and gave my best rendition. Although I had practiced this many times, at home under Lorien's tutelage, and then again this morning during breaks and free periods, I was nervous. I was no Lorien. I managed to get through it painlessly, and hopefully only I noticed the couple of clinkers I let go throughout the piece. I knew she was going to hate it though. I knew she would point her finger at me and scream 'PLAGIARIST!' with my class echoing her. I was no Lorien.

However, Mrs Lawper stood and started to clap. The class did join her, to my delight, not embarrassment. I still knew I was a fake. Yes, I could have done this myself. Perhaps not to the level of Lorien's embellished work, but still completed - justly, suitably and even well. And, as always, when flustered, my blush tried to again reveal my lie. Mrs Lawper read it as being humble though, thank God. "That was brilliant Mrs Standish!" Mrs Lawper said, walking up to the piano, and dropping her hand causally over the side, checking out the sheet-music. Was she looking for tell-tales of Lorien? Would she know? I started to panic again. "I have never heard such enthusiasm for a school song before, and I have taught at quite a few." She dropped me a quick smile, and continued. "Do you think it may be a little 'large' for Sommersett though?" Yes, yes, yes! She had my total agreement. But my mouth did not respond, my hands did. I stood and tore the manuscript in half. Her face was shocked, but I only smiled at her. My mouth finally unzipped.

"I couldn't agree with you more Mrs Lawper, it was way too overdone. I had my suspicions as it was written, but couldn't seem to stop." She laughed, loudly, head thrown back.

"I wish you hadn't ripped it up though Mrs Standish, it is still a wonderful piece, and one that could be used for more formal pomp and circumstance, like graduation ceremonies and such." She was right, of course. I felt like an absolute dramatic twit. This thought now making me say,

"A little dramatic of me?" She just smiled and patted my shoulder.

"We can discuss this further at another time less inconvenient to your students. And although a little more than I was expecting, am very happy with your submission." With that, she turned on her heel, leaving the room.

I decided to work back a little that evening, for several reasons. Once the bell rang to signal the end of the student's day, I closed the doors and sat at my desk, debating on where to start. The sigh I emitted came from the very depth of my soul; I had so much paperwork to get through. As a rule, I would take it home and finish it there, but the papers I was marking today were compositions and I had to be able to play them physically to mark them. It was more practical to do it in the music room than at home with the distractions. I also had a school song to redo.

Lost in my own world at the piano, my mobile rang. It was Lorien. I was not disappointed. "Hey Baby, how come you're so late?"

"Hi Honey, I'm trying to get the marking done, I'll be home as soon as I can."

"Do you realise it's nearly 6 o'clock?" I hadn't. The thought didn't thrill me any. I needed to get this done and I was still only about halfway through the marking.

"Lorien, I am going to be here until it's finished. Can you look after Mercy? I'll be home as soon as I can," I reiterated.

"Sure Baby. Do you want me to help?"

"No thanks, I know how much work *wouldn't* get done if you were to come and 'help me'," I chided. I heard him chuckle lowly. He then told me he loved me and would see me soon.

It was hard to get back on track once the phone call ended. My thoughts took me back to when Lorien had worked here the two weeks Alan O'Dowd took off on leave. Lorien had waggled the music room keys at me several times, wanting me to join him up here for a blissful afternoon once school had finished. I was heavily pregnant at the time, so it never ended up happening, unfortunately. These pleasant musings were not helping me get through my workload though, and I forced myself back to the piano.

At 8.30, I checked my watch, surprised again, at how long I had been sitting here. Mercy would be asleep by now and dinner eaten, cleaned up, and forgotten. I was down to the last half dozen assignments and decided the school song would have to wait. I stretched and stood, my spine protesting briefly at the change in position. I needed a coffee, and I headed into the little kitchenette off the music room to make it.

My spoon froze as I heard the soft melody come floating in from the music room. I recognised it at once, it was 'Ashlyn's Song', and I knew my husband was now sitting at the piano in the adjoining room. I didn't know whether to let him come and find me, or to interrupt him by walking in. He knew I was here somewhere as the lights were on and obviously, the door was unlocked. I let him get nearly all the way through before I went to join him, a warm smile on my face.

He looked up as I entered, and the same smile broke out on his face. I sat next to him on the piano bench as he played out the last few notes, then turned to kiss me.

"What are you doing here?" I asked quietly, so not to break the mood.

"Fulfilling a fantasy," he said and leant in to kiss me again. I had no intention of stopping him. Movement was rather constricted on the narrow bench, so I stood and Lorien rose with me. One arm wended around my waist, drawing me near, as the other reached up and closed the top lid of the upright piano. I was then hoisted into the air, landing adroitly on the closed lid.

"What are you planning, with me up here?" I asked coyly. His reply was a flashing grin. He snaked his hands up the length of my thighs, coming to rest on the waistband of my briefs. As he drew them down, I understood his purpose.

"Lay back Baby," he crooned, and I did so gladly. He then pulled me forward by the hip, putting my calves on his shoulders, then sealing his mouth to me. Being at this elevation, he didn't have to bend far to reach.

One thing neither of us calculated was the restricted ledge of the piano lid teemed with my gratified writhing. As I went to topple off, Lorien grabbed my waist on either side, steadying me. It was a close call. "Oops," he said and laughed, and I sat up and hugged him to me. I had been so very close, and was not in the mood to laugh. With my legs wrapped around his sides, I stayed straddled as I kissed him in full fervour.

He slid me forward and carried me to my desk, laying me over it and hitching up to join me on its platform. His blunt tip made me gasp as he forced me open, taking me in one hard thrust. This rhythm did not last long however as I couldn't help but laugh at the rat-a-tat of the uneven desk legs on the floor. Humour enveloped me at the weirdest and most inappropriate times on occasion.

"Ash," he laugh-groaned.

"I can't help it Lorien," I said in a more serious tone, then spoilt it with a giggle. He climbed off me and then the table, and I sat up, curious to see how he would solve this problem. And solve it, he did, and in record time.

Lorien pulled the piano cover off the cupboard top, nicely quilted in a decor from long ago, and shoved some student desks and chairs out of the way before spreading it on the floor. I went to him, and yet another record was broken.

When the pulsing eased, he flumped on his side beside me, pulling me close. "I love you," he said softly, his breath still irregular, as was mine. I rolled toward him and purred into his ear, confirming my love for him as well. He chuckled shortly after, removing his busy fingers from inside me and feeding their wetness into his mouth. "Someone needs a cleanup." He decided to take care of that personally and dove down, tickling at the back of my knees as he went for gold.

I loved making love to Lorien; my body beating alongside the love I had for him in my heart.

Mark Up

"There is no amount of pain,
To make me forget your name."

L Standish, 'More Than Skin Deep'

I AWOKE BEFORE LORIEN and watched *him* sleep for a change. It was usually the other way around. I wanted to ask him something, and it was difficult not to wake him, but I restrained myself. Finally, his deep brown eyes fluttered slowly open. "This is a nice change," he said, "you watching me," then lowered me to him for a kiss.

"I wanted to ask you something, and have for some time," I blurted out. He rubbed his eyes and sat up a little.

"You have my full attention."

"I was just wondering..." Here I went again, unable to speak openly to him about the things we do. What was wrong with me? After all these years, I *still* had issues with it. I sighed and he smiled at me with encouragement. "Well... I wanted to know how you could do what you did last night." He looked confused and then alarmed.

"I didn't hurt you?" he asked, now sitting up fully.

"No, nothing like that," I said and kissed him lightly before snuggling into him so I could hide my face. "But you... tasted yourself... on me..." He chuckled and hugged me tightly.

"I don't see my bashful Angel as often as I used to, but it is still nice to see." He played his fingers lightly over my back in a soft caress, before continuing to speak. "You do it too, you know."

"When?" I asked in disbelief.

"When I kiss you after I've gone down on you." His crudity sent a flash through my body. Lorien was hardly a foul-mouth in the bedroom, but he knew how I would react to his words. His hand was already edging over my stomach, heading for the warm space between my thighs. And he kissed me, working me magically until I groaned into his mouth. To add to his answer, he kissed his way down my body, teasing my nipples with his tongue before letting it find his final destination. And when he had coaxed a second tremor through me, lay across my lap looking up at me, smiling. "Come here," he said and gestured with his finger before entwining them through my hair and drawing my lips down to his, finalising the act with a deep kiss. I realised I didn't mind at all.

Life had gone on as usual pretty much, for most of us. I myself had been enjoying the casual placement as the music teacher at Sommersett High. Since Alan O'Dowd retired, I had been backfilling the vacancy, and if there was any truth to the rumour, it was about to be externally advertised. I could only dare hope for my success. Not that we needed the money, but I did need a job, or face going insane. Being less than a minute's walk from home was also a bonus. Lorien had continued to gain quiet success with his music. He was currently under contract to write jingles for an extensive new ad campaign for a large potato chip manufacturer. He hated jingles, but it was easy work with an excellent financial return. His latest personal project though was immense in its complexity in comparison to the jingle writing. He had started working on a modern rock opera about six months ago - words and music by Lorien Thomas Standish. I admired him so much for his enthusiasm; if I were faced with the daunting endless task, I would have tossed it aside long ago. Like maybe five and a half months ago.

Lorien, however, thrived on this kind of challenge. He would play snippets for me from time to time to get my input and advice. I had asked why he wouldn't play me an entire piece, or verbalise the lyrics for one completely penned song, regardless of the melody not having been finished. He hadn't completed any, was his response. He was literally working in fragments. I knew once he had created enough, when spliced together to form the entire rainbow of ideals, it would be magical. And Elijah...

Elijah was still working with Dr Wood at the local surgery, assisting at the Emergency Ward at Byrong Hospital when required. He had decided long ago that this was where his preference lay. He wasn't interested in grabbing handfuls of money, as was a likely possibility in being a Specialist, but was content to look after his local community. And, was a well-respected member of Sommersett, as were we all, I supposed. At times though, I felt a little way-sided in comparison to the successful, enthused twins. Lorien called me silly and social standing, in Sommersett or any other town, was hardly something to aspire over.

A soft knock at the door brought me from my musings. We expected it to be Elijah, and were both surprised to see a coy Mercy, once Lorien had called to come in. We shared a smiling glance before Lorien lifted her onto the bed to snuggle between us. "I'm very excited," she gushed, wriggling her way further under the covers. Castlebrook Show was on this weekend and we both knew what she was referring to, but feigned ignorance.

"And why is that Merce?" Lorien asked.

"It's Saturday! We're going to the Show!"

"Oh, right," he said. "How could have I forgotten?" Mercy tsked at her father and gave him a disapproving look. What a silly Daddy! It was all she had talked about since Christmas; it wasn't likely we would have been allowed to forget. She wasn't even fully aware of what attending 'the Show' even entailed. I guessed she had picked it up at day-care.

"Is Unkie Lie awake?" I asked.

"Nuh." Mercy would more often than not make her first stop of the morning in Elijah's bed. On the rare occasion Lorien and I would arise before him, we would sneak the door open and warm our hearts on the vision of the two spoons huddled together. A serving spoon and a teaspoon no less, but Mercy loved her Uncle so much, and he in return loved her as much, if not more. I wished he would find someone to love, to have kids with, to spend a life creating together. He deserved it.

My melancholy sigh drew Lorien's attention, and I smiled and shook my head at him. It was nothing we needed to speak of. And I knew Lorien held the same hopes for Elijah as I did.

As soon as the sound of a toilet flushing reached Mercy's ears, she climbed out from under the covers, stood up and bounced her way off our bed. She knew Unkie Lie was up. "Come on, let's go!" She dragged on her father's arm for a few seconds without success, and when she realised he wasn't getting up, tried another tactic. Hands on hips, eyes fixed in a stubborn glower, she raised her left foot, ready to stomp.

"If that foot hits the ground, young lady, we will not be going anywhere," I threatened. I finished this with a light punch to Lorien's arm, who was currently trying to hide a smirk. We got out of bed though, and I rang Michael to confirm times with him.

We decided to take the train, as there was a station right near the showground. Mercy had also never been on one, and she knelt on the seat and watched out the window for the entire 35-minute ride. A five-minute walk later, we were queuing up to pay our admission. The prices had gone up again this year and I knew that the rides would be even worse, let alone the showbags. Oh well, it was a once-a-year event, and we were all looking forward to it. When Mercy was older, we might even consider upgrading her to the Royal Easter Show in Sydney. Might...

The first thing Mercy wanted was fairy floss. The five men also decided on a Pluto pup and some hot chips; Bree and I settled on a snow cone each. I knew the dangers of eating show food and then getting on the rides. This wasn't a problem for Bree though, as she was always the official bag holder. She was a wuss when it came to thrills and chills, hopefully not spills.

Elijah, Simon, Glen and Michael all took off shortly after to go in search of the newest rides, leaving Lorien, Bree, myself and Mercy to start with the kiddie stuff. Sideshow alley, here we come.

When younger, I was always impressed by having a boyfriend who could win you crap on the laughing clowns and such, and it came in handy, now having a child who wanted the same. Lorien won her a panda on the ring toss, a ceramic vase (her choice) on the basketball hoops and she won herself a 24-carat gold necklace on the clowns. Every child wins a prize! Mercy placed it around her neck, and I was sure she'd have a lovely green ring at her throat to show for it within an hour. With each alternative game, she once again ate: popcorn, waffle cone, more fairy floss. I didn't know where she kept putting it.

We were a little selective about what rides she was allowed on, and even Bree accompanied us. The carousel, ferris wheel, chair swings, house of mirrors and dodgem cars were all successfully navigated without incident. I said no though when she wanted to go on the ghost train. "I'll take her Ash, it's only the ghost train," Lorien said.

"No Honey, she's way too young." I myself had not gone on the ghost train, or in the haunted house until I was well into my teens. Maybe Bree wasn't the wuss after all, perhaps it was me.

"I want to find the Big machine," Mercy interrupted, now over her flight of fancy with the train that disappeared out of sight. I don't think she knew what she was asking for when wanting to ride it initially, until she heard the word 'ghost' come out of Lorien's mouth.

"What's the Big machine?" Bree asked with a smile, hoisting her up onto her hip. Mercy wended her little arms around her Aunty Bree's neck, and we started to walk aimlessly through the fairway. Bree looked at me and I shrugged my shoulders. I had no idea what she was referring to either.

"You know, the BIG machine!" She couldn't explain herself any better than that. Lorien then barked out a laugh, realising what she was getting at.

"Do you mean the fortune teller booth from the movie 'Big'?" He confirmed.

"Yes." We all laughed, and Mercy's face took on a look of thunder. "What's so funny!"

"Merce, that's only in a movie, it doesn't exist in real life."

"But I want to be big!"

"You'll get there soon enough," I sighed.

We ran into the guys about twenty minutes later, all hotted up and full of adrenalin. They had obviously found what they went looking for. "Is she exhausted yet?" Michael asked me, taking Mercy from Bree and swinging her up onto his shoulders. She laughed and giggled, loving the attention from Uncle Michael. Always.

"No," she answered for me.

"Ready for some adult stuff Mum?" he asked. And Mercy replied for me again,

"Yes!"

"Uncle Michael was talking to me Merce, not you." She didn't seem to care.

We found ourselves standing in front of the Gravitron and Mercy was allowed to go in it with her Uncles. She felt so grown up. Lorien decided against it, and told me he'd be back shortly, and then disappeared into the crowd. So, Bree and I waited outside with the haul. Mercy's face was flushed when it finished.

We hung around for about half an hour watching the human zoo pass us by. I was also waiting on Lorien's return. "Want to eat yet?" Simon asked, meaning lunch.

"I want to go on the rides first and eat after, I'll be sick otherwise," I answered. "I need to find Lorien first though." I couldn't go on the rides without him, and mere seconds later, he came bursting through the crowd, puffed from running. "Where have you been?" I asked. He carried nothing so I was unsure exactly what he had been doing.

"All in good time Baby," he said and dropped me a wink, as his arm draped over my shoulders. Elijah snorted and shook his head, and I glanced at him, one eyebrow raised, in question. He turned away so I checked out the faces on the other three gents, but they seemed unaware of the entire interaction between the twins. I knew *something* was going on, or had been.

And then the adult stuff began. Bree waited with Mercy as we had our fill on the Giant Drop, Hurricane, Pirate Ship, Octopus, Rollercoaster and the Zipper. I was more of a 'tried and tested' kind of girl, opting for the better-known rides. I also had a hidden vein of worry when on these rides, knowing fatalities had occurred in the past with fire and mechanical failure. I'd always been uncertain whether the likes of theme parks, where the rides were not dismantled, was safer, or whether the constant pull down and reconstruct was the better choice. You would think that they'd notice any damage when being handled every week. I actually rang WorkSafety a few years ago to ask that very question and was told the Amusement Parks won hands down. All that travel with the equipment rattling around, things became loose or eroded. I hadn't thought of that. I wish I hadn't thought of it now either, as we were not currently at an Amusement Park. The chances were slim, and I didn't let myself get caught up on it. The look of the carnies running the rides was more of a concern.

When arriving safely at the bottom of the Giant Drop, I realised my nervous worries as an adult about the mechanical safety of the rides was not expressed on the faces of the teens who were disembarking with us. It took me back to my youth, recalling how the thrill of these rides was as close as you got to understanding the thrill of sex and all it contained, when you were still too young to comprehend the impact. I recalled getting off a similar thrill ride when in my early teens, face flushed, pulse racing, feeling like I was on top of the world. How similar I now felt after a lovemaking session with my Lorien. Flushed, pulsing, elated. I then laughed, knowing all these kids felt like they had just had sex, but not understanding that.

We ate, and I had a Pluto pup this time too. Couldn't go to the Show without one! Mercy also insisted on having one, and tomato sauce covered her fingers and face. It was the best way to enjoy a Pluto pup though. Good for her.

Cleaned up, we headed for the showbags, which was our last stop before going home. None of us wanted to lug them around with us all day. Mercy was told she could have no more than five, and decided on the My Little Doll and Magic Fun showbags, and the Smarties, Bertie Beetle and Snakes Alive options. I went with my usual Smith's Crisps and Nestlé, and the guys loaded up with several each. Such sweet tooths.

"Aww," Michael complained, "no packet of Ollo's in them anymore!" This was an old joke as Ollo's chips weren't in the showbags when we were younger either. Did they even make them anymore? It was doubtful.

On the way back to the entrance, Mercy stopped by the Sizzler, which I considered an adult ride. Sure, it didn't go up and down at a speedy rate, but it did go around and around. "Pleeeeease Mummy!" she begged, tugging at my jeans.

"Merce, you'll be sick." I had noted that she had said 'Mummy' though and not Baby, making sure she was on her best behaviour when begging.

"I'll take her if you like," Elijah offered. I looked at Lorien and he smiled.

"Let her Mummy, this one's not so bad." I relented, unwisely.

About three quarters of the way through the ride, Mercy's face went from grey to green to red. She tried, to no avail, to beat the centrifugal force by putting her hand to her mouth, but was unable to stop it. The popcorn, fairy floss, waffle cone and Pluto pup came spewing out of her mouth in a viscous brown pulse. Elijah looked horrified.

When the ride stopped, Elijah brought a crying Mercy to us by the hand, then stripped off his shirt and threw it into a nearby bin. He was lucky that was the only piece of clothing affected. "I'm sorry Unkie Lie!" Mercy howled.

"It's OK Merce, look, I'm vomit-free now," he said and laughed as he scooped her into his arms. The acidic smell that only a child's vomit can convey still hung mildly in the air, and I assumed she had splashed him elsewhere. It wasn't overpowering though, but I did a quick search through her hair.

She cheered up on the train ride, going through her Magic showbag with Uncle Simon. She got us all in her trickery with the Whoopie Cushion and Snappy Gum; we were so easily fooled! The fake hickey tattoo cracked us all up the most. It had been a wonderful day at the Castlebrook Show, but I was glad it was over.

As we alighted at Sommersett station, Simon threw his arm around Lorien's shoulders, laughing at whatever they had been discussing. Lorien drew back instantly and winced. "Serves you right!" Elijah scoffed, and I handed Mercy to Michael, stepping in front of Lorien.

"What?" was my simple question. The others, unaware of current proceedings, kept walking. Everyone, other than Elijah.

"Nothing," Lorien answered, moving his left shoulder away from me. I don't think he even realised he was doing it.

"Are you hurt?" I asked, again searching for the problem. He didn't answer right away, and I started to feel concern growing in the pit of my stomach. *Had he dislocated something on one of those stupid rides? Fallen over or into something, and being the hero, kept it to himself? But why wouldn't he have told Elijah, he could have helped. Wait! Elijah seems to know what's going on...* All through these musings which took place in less than two seconds, our crowd had stopped walking, and came back to circle loosely around we three. Their curiosity had been aroused and Michael hated to miss a thing. Glen, possibly sensing the air of danger that was developing, took Mercy from Michael and continued a short way up the platform, stopping to look at the yellow 'piss-flowers' that grew along the entire train-line cutting through the eastern coast of Australia. They were less than spectacular.

"It's a surprise," Lorien relented and handed me this tidbit, knowing that it would not be enough.

"Try again," I told him, my hands finding their way to my hips. Perhaps this is where Mercy had learnt the pose.

"In a week Baby, I promise."

"Now Lorien!" I was worried, and a little scared, but only a little. I knew if it were anything massive, Elijah would have intervened by now. So, I cast my glare at Elijah.

"I told him not to do it at that dingy hole," Elijah offered.

"Do what?!" I found my voice was rising and sounded a little shrill. I again looked at Lorien.

"Way to dob me in bro," Lorien laughed then faced me. He sighed, then pulled up his T-Shirt sleeve and gently removed the medical pad. An unseen Simon whistled between his teeth before bellowing out a laugh.

"You dick Lorien," he said, then laughed again. "That looks like Mercy drew it!" He was enjoying this way too much.

"Ermagerd twin!" was all Michael could get out, and through my peripheral vision, saw Michael turn to face me, waiting silently on my reaction. Unable to hold himself though, he added, "You got this for your mother?" He also joined Simon; now the laughing duo. Bree never said a word.

"Knock it off," Elijah told them, suspecting my response was not going to be great. His warning went unheeded and the two of them continued to bray out their laughter. Lorien had gone slightly red, and the heat of the day had nothing to do with it.

Glen called out to Mercy, who had run back to us wanting to know what was so funny, and Lorien quickly pulled his sleeve down, a little too roughly. He grimaced and then laughed weakly, unable to stop himself as the co-conspirators of mirth egged him on.

"What's so funny?" Mercy asked, standing in front of Michael and Simon.

"Nothing Honey," Elijah answered, picking her up. "It's an adult thing." Mercy tsked, having heard this more often than once, when it was not a suitable discussion or joke for her young ears. She teamed it with an eye-roll at her Uncle, which set the giggling fools off again. We headed for home, with still no comment from me.

Bree filled Mercy's inflatable pool whilst Michael and Simon took a seat on the verandah, the twins going to source a few refreshing beers. Glen and I helped Bree drag the pool into the shade as the quiet laughter continued to bubble, with the occasional heard word.

"He's in for it," said one, unknown to me from this distance. Then mumbles. "Doghouse for sure!" Then more laughter and further muted conversation.

I stripped Mercy off to the buff and motioned for Michael to toss me the sunscreen. He managed to pass it down to me, still laughing, and eyes drilling into me, waiting on my final comments to be laid out in front of them - for Simon and Michael's amusement, no doubt. I thanked him and smiled sweetly, telling him he was a fool.

Mercy took the 'Christ on the Cross' position and I sprayed her, front and back, before Bree, Glen and I joined the idiots on the verandah. Splash! Mercy was otherwise entertained for a good half an hour now.

As I climbed the stairs Elijah came out with the beers and Lorien flicked on the radio, taking a seat, taking a beer, and holding his arms out to me, wanting me to settle on his knee. He smiled impishly at me.

I took the seat next to him, more concerned about hurting him, than being pissed with him. "Well?" he asked, popping the top off a Corona and handing it to me. I sipped slowly and finally, the laughter died. All eyes were upon me.

"Would you care to show me again?" I asked. Lorien gently pulled his T-Shirt over his head and angled his shoulder toward me so I could better see his new tattoo. "You had this done by a carny?" I asked quietly.

"It's OK Ash," Elijah piped up. "I will keep my eye on it." I nodded to show I had heard him but did not remove my gaze from the inking. I brushed my finger over it gently, then pulled back abruptly, not wanting to hurt Lorien.

"I'm fine Baby," he confirmed, and delicately placed my finger against the outline once again. He had a bass clef tattooed on his left shoulder, about five centimetres high. At its base was an M and an A on either side of the downward swirl. My finger traced over the initials softly, and Michael responded with,

"Ma! Where's my Ma?" I had to chuckle with him, realising what he had been on about, when asking whether this had been done for his mother. I also had to agree with Simon. It wasn't the most professional tattoo I had ever seen, and I was *such* an expert, but it seemed rather infantile insofar as how it had been etched. The lines *were* a little sloppy.

"I told you she'd kill you," Elijah said quietly. They were still waiting on my reaction, and they had been so patient.

I pressed my lips softly to Lorien's, taking his face into my hands. When I drew back, he looked at me warily, still not knowing where this was going. "I love it Honey," I whispered into his ear. And I did. The ideal of what this represented was so true of our love, and the love of our daughter. My eyes started to burn lightly before a small trickle of tears found their way from my lids, down my cheeks. I lowered my face, not wanting the others to see, but a single finger lifted my chin as Lorien brushed them away with his thumb.

"I love you Ashlyn," he whispered back, then kissed me with intent.

"How the *hell* did he get out of *that* one?" I heard Simon ask no one in particular, making us break our kiss, laughing.

Lorien put his shirt back on before Mercy got out of the pool. This was not something she needed to see immediately, and certainly not before it had a chance to heal. Kids with their poking fingers of curiosity could be a danger in any household.

A few more beers, a barbeque and my love growing impossibly deeper for Lorien took place over the next few hours. I felt my face soften every time our eyes met, not being able to comprehend how much I could actually love this man. Each time I thought I had reached what was possibly a peak of our love, he went and one-upped me. I loved him so much for it.

Around 9 o'clock, our guests said their goodbyes. We would see them tomorrow, with an afternoon at Glassread to be enjoyed by all. As was often the case these days, the weekends went by in a whirlwind of commotion, keeping us all close, involved and active. I loved my life!

Taking Instruction

"And when I think you've done it all
You go out and surprise me."

L Standish, 'Further Education'

WHEN OPENING THE PLANTATION SHUTTERS the next morning, I saw the beautiful day that awaited us. We were sure to have a great afternoon. "What time is it Baby?" Lorien yawned, rolling onto his back and stretching.

"A little after eight."

"Coming back to bed for a while?" he asked, running his hands down under the sheets, giving me a fair idea of his intentions.

"Merce will want her breakfast."

"Let Eli do it," he answered and sat up, leaning forward toward me, his arms outstretched. He winced.

"She's *our* daughter Honey," I said and frowned at him, then smiled and leant down to kiss him. "Still hurts?" I asked in all naivety. I had no idea how long it took for the sting to be removed from a new tattoo. He chose to ignore my question, having more pressing issues at hand.

"Come on, just a little longer." That little longer took a further forty minutes. I was also very careful to avoid his newly acquired artwork.

Mercy was sitting at the dining room table having her breakfast with Unkie Lie when we made it downstairs. I eyed the weird looking harlequin concoction they were eating before asking, "What is that?"

"Beetroot and grilled cheese on toast," Elijah answered.

"You're kidding me."

"Nope. Want one?"

"Ah, no thanks," I murmured, feeling a little grossed out. Lorien smiled at me from the sink where he was whipping together the ingredients for an omelette.

"It's been one of Eli's favourites since we were little, you should try it," he advised.

"I see *you're* not having one," I accused.

"I said it was one of Eli's favourites, not mine," he laughed, and went back to whisking the eggs.

"It's yummy, Mummy," Mercy said and grinned, her tiny pearls now a lovely shade of violet.

"Uncle Simon would love it," I told her and barely repressed a shudder, remembering his sandwiches from early high school; a purple and yellow sodden mass by lunchtime. At least the colours were complementary to each other as far as the colour-spectrum was concerned.

I sat at the table next to Mercy and planted a kiss on her forehead. Fortunately, she was in a position where I couldn't see her colourful mouth. She was humming to herself and swinging her feet under the table, licking up the beetroot juice that had run down her arm. Elijah chuckled and I looked up at him as Lorien slid a plate in front of me. Their eyes obviously met, as then they chuckled together and I turned around to face Lorien, raising my eyebrows in question to their mirth. "Nothing Baby," he said and sat opposite me.

"We're going to Glassread today Mummy?" Mercy asked.

"Yes Sweetie, Uncles Michael and Glen will meet us there around eleven," I confirmed as I cut into my omelette and was just about to fork it into my mouth when I noticed the eerie silence coming from the twins.

"What?" I asked. They both smiled and shook their heads. I then shook mine back at them - such foolery on such a beautiful morning.

It was when I looked down at the fork poised to enter my mouth, I understood the hilarity. Lorien had layered the bottom of the omelette with beetroot slices. "Oh... you!" was the best I could get out under the circumstances. I had to laugh with them though, as I stood, ready to dump it into the garbage.

"Try it at least," Elijah suggested.

"It's not too bad Ash," Lorien agreed through a mouthful. I took a small hesitant bite, and although not the foulest thing I had ever eaten, it was not something I wanted for breakfast today.

"No, I'll have cereal," I conceded and moved toward the bin.

"I'll eat it," Elijah said and took the plate from my hand as I passed.

"It's all yours."

Michael and Glen hadn't arrived when we got there. I took care of disassembling Mercy from her car seat whilst the twins picked a spot and set up the rugs and eskies. Michael and Glen arrived a few minutes later, the twins already stripped down to their board-shorts. "Hi kids," Michael greeted us, and Mercy dove at him. He swung her around before lifting her into his arms for a hug. "How's my favourite girl doing?"

"I'm OK," I answered. Mercy frowned at me and Michael laughed.

"He means me Mummy!" she reprimanded.

"Silly me!" I said and felt Lorien's arms slip around me from behind.

"You're still *my* favourite girl," he whispered into my ear.

"Shh! Mercy will hear you," I said, turning to face him. Mercy had this thing, as most three year olds did I assumed, about being the centre of everyone's universe. We didn't help either, by making it so.

"I think she's aware that we're rather fond of each other," he said and smiled before leaning in to kiss me.

"Who's swimming?" Glen asked.

"Me! Me!" Mercy squealed and wriggled from Michael's grip. She grabbed Lorien by the hand, "Come on Orrie," and tried to drag him toward the baths. Obviously, she couldn't budge him, and he stood his ground, turning it into a game. "ORRIE!" she stormed, ready to turn this into a tantrum. She hated not getting her way. Lorien bent down to her level and pulled her close.

"Daddy is my name."

"Come on Daddy!" she then whined, still pulling futilely on his arm.

"You will wait until the grownups are ready young lady. If you start making a fuss, there will be no swimming!" As soft as Lorien was with her, he was also wonderful at pulling her into line when needed. Mercy pouted and let go of Lorien's hand, flumping onto the ground with her arms and legs crossed in front of her. Lorien walked away, letting her sit there and stew for a few minutes. The twins were ready for a swim too, as was Glen, so she wouldn't have to sit there for long. Faint memories of my own childhood washed in front of my eyes, reminding me that five minutes once felt like an hour. Still, she had to learn.

We all caught up for a few moments, Mercy finally relenting, realising she wasn't going to get her way and re-joined us on the rugs, her face now a smile instead of a scowl as she climbed onto her father's lap. Her moods didn't last long, thank God. And shortly thereafter, they all headed toward the baths, leaving me and Michael alone. "Not swimming?" I asked.

"I have a pool at home, why would I want to swim in that gunk!" I smiled broadly, then laughed, knowing how adverse Michael was to mud and lake weed. It was hardly like going to the beach.

"Sook," I teased.

"I see you're not going in?" he threw back.

"The painters are due." Michael pulled a face, and asked,

"What?"

"My period is due," I said, and laughed when he pulled another face at me.

We talked for a while about nothing and everything, and as always, the subject soon turned to sex. I was glad this time, as there was something I wanted to ask him. I was full of questions of late. I knew by putting myself out there I could be the brunt of Michael's playful side, but trusted when I was serious, he would come up with the goods.

"Michael..." I started.

"Yeeeeeeeeees," he drawled.

"Can I ask you something?"

"Is it about gay sex?" he asked and laughed.

"Well, no, not really. It's to do with me..."

"I'm all ears," he gushed and sat up, moving closer to me to make the conversation more intimate.

"Michael..." I warned.

"I promise to be on my best adult behaviour!" I had heard *that* one before. "Come on Ash, I promise to behave."

"Well..." I started and lowered my eyes.

"This oughta be good, you're blushing already." He lifted my chin with one finger and looked me in the eyes. We both ended up laughing.

When the humour bubble burst and we'd regained our composure I started again, but through a different angle. "You're a man, right."

"Last time I checked," he said and only smiled, not wanting to interrupt me, or put me off.

"What do you like?"

"Sexually?"

"Yes." He looked at me and drew in one eyebrow, possibly confused as to my point. "All men are men, regardless of their chosen sexual preference, correct?"

"Sure."

"Then what you enjoy, *any* man would."

"Well, to a degree Ash, but I can't imagine your twin would like you coming at him with a strap-on." This broke us both up again into peals of laughter.

"You understand what I mean though?"

"Yeah, but every man is also different, as are women I assume. Where you like to be touched and caressed may not be the same as Bree. Have you had this conversation with her?"

"No, I never thought about it." I sighed, knowing this was not as cut and dried as I first assumed it would be.

"Surely you're not having trouble in the sack?"

"No," I said and smiled. "It's just that he does so many wonderful things for me, *to* me, and I wanted to give him something a little more."

"I've never heard him complain."

"I know, it's just..." I didn't know how to end that sentence.

"You want something out of left field? Something a woman may not think to do for a man? Something he may not even realise could be enjoyed?"

"Yes, exactly." I was glad he was on my wavelength.

"What level are his boundaries?" Michael was now taking this seriously and we started on the twenty questions.

"What do *you* reckon?" I said and laughed.

"No, I can't imagine he wouldn't let you do anything to him you wanted."

"No," I said and blushed again... damn it!

"Ever heard of rimming?" I laughed aloud at this.

"Lorien used to massage my perineum when I was pregnant to lessen the chance of tearing."

"That's hardly the same thing."

"He also offered that, but I declined."

"You declined..." he mused and grinned at me.

"I don't think I could do that to him though Michael, it sort of grosses me out."

"OK. Maybe I need to start with *your* boundaries then." Yes, maybe he should...

I could hear Mercy calling to me and I looked up to see her running back to the rug, the three men not far behind her. "Oh great, we just get to the nitty gritty and here they come," I groaned.

"Later Babe," Michael said and winked, opening his arms for Mercy to land in. "And you need to work on that blush madam; our conversation is written all over your face," he whispered to me. It didn't help that Lorien was wet from the waist down, and his towel, as were the other's, was slung around his neck. As they neared, the trees dappled their shadows over him, luring my eyes to the strength of his chest, shoulders and abs. The sight of him still did it for me, even after three years of marriage, not to mention our passionate youth.

In true male form, all three of them wound their towels around their waists and stripped off the wet boardies from underneath, draping them over the bough of a nearby tree to dry. Lorien then straddled over my lap and opened the towel, wrapping it around us both. As he kissed me, he lowered me onto my back, and I fought senselessly against him; he far outweighed me. "Lorien," I mumbled, trying not to laugh.

"She's three, she's got no idea," he breathed and deepened the kiss.

"Lorien," I said, moving my mouth away from his, "there are other people here too!" *Yeah, good luck with that!* Michael mouthed at me, assuming there was nothing he could say that would improve what we already had. For once though, Lorien minded me and propped himself up on his elbows, running the contours of my face with his finger as he smiled lazily down at me. I couldn't help but smile back.

"Daddy's got a picture on his arm, Mummy!" Mercy chirped, climbing onto Lorien's back, forcing their combined weight onto me.

"Off! Both of you!" I called, and Lorien rose up, taking their weight with his shoulders. He had forgotten one was rather sore! He wrapped his good arm around the back of Mercy and shifted to his side, keeping her on board, but moving off me. This allowed me to slide out from under him, and then Mercy to slide off the back of him. She thought it hilarious and wanted to go again. "Why are you half dry?" I asked him, Mercy now trotting off to see what her Uncles were doing. Lorien's 'picture' was dismissed for now.

"Can't get the tattoo wet yet Baby," Lorien replied.

"Oh." I didn't know the ins and outs of new tattoos and from the look of this one, had no intention of finding out. It was getting crusty and was a little red. Elijah told me it was normal though. It would soon crust up completely and would heal soon after. I smiled and shook my head, drawing my finger lightly over the outline again. Lorien lay there contented, watching me.

There was nothing wrong with Mercy's hearing. She came skipping back to us, chanting "Wet yet. Wet yet. Wet yet." Her forgotten interest in her Daddy's picture had been renewed. "Will it wash off?" She asked Lorien.

"No," he answered.

"Can I have one?"

"*No!*" we answered in unison, then laughed.

"How did you get it?" she finally asked after a few seconds of staring at it, her little nose about five centimetres away from it.

"It's a bit like a sewing machine," Lorien explained. "A little needle goes up and down putting ink just under my skin, so it stays there." During this explanation he was doing the visuals with his hands to show her.

"Does it hurt?" she asked, sticking her pointer finger roughly against it.

"Yes," Lorien gasped, scuttering away from the needle-like finger of his three year old. He gave the tattoo a light rub and told her not to do that again. She minded.

"It looks weird," was her final statement, clueless that she had possibly physically hurt her Dad, or that he was a little mad at her. She went to join her Uncles once again. And these Uncles were all sitting there, grinning at us. I gave them the finger, and their grins became a laugh.

Lorien quizzed me on the way home about work, getting the 'inside goss' on what had been happening and with whom. Yes, the old fridge in the staff room was still a heap of wheezing garbage, small, unreliable and here for the time being. Janet Kowalenko was still there, working as the ceramics teacher but I didn't have to deal with 'Mr' Turner, who Lorien knew well. Mr Turner was previously another Music teacher at Sommersett - old, stuffy and in desperate need of a lesson in personal space. Lorien laughed, remembering his own issues in tossing Mr Turner's desk contents back onto his own side of the adjoining Music teacher's desks. Lorien liked to use a ruler shoved in between the two desks to serve as a boundary reminder. I was not so assertive. And thankfully, Andrew Dean was now in his place. As for the other two teachers that shared our staffroom, the Commercial Printmaking role was currently vacant, and Karen Smith was the Art teacher.

Karen was a quiet young woman who also doubled as a dance tutor to those who wished to pursue that through their lunchtime or after school. I think that was Karen's passion in life, although she was an excellent artist and knew her theory and craft. Lorien and I had discussed Mercy taking lessons outside of school, but were still undecided. I thought it best to leave it until Mercy showed some talent, or asked to do it, but Lorien thought the idea of a little girl in ballet tutus and such, was a sweet thing. Let's face it though, an all-day concert is the end result of her taking lessons. That meant watching God knows how many similar dances by the same aged little girls around the Region, all with the same dance. *Arms up! Point toe out and tap it on the ground. Spin around. Repeat.* Watching three year olds, without much talent, dance, was like watching test match cricket on the television. Many would disagree with me, but many would not!

"Oh!" Mercy interjected from the back seat. "Ms Smith is going to be my dance teacher!" she informed us. How did Mercy know who Karen

Smith even was? She did not let us consider that for too long, bursting into an excited account of how Jade and Jaimie were now taking Karen's dance classes. I looked at Lorien and rolled my eyes. He laughed and took my hand, placing it on his thigh. We would deal with this when we had to I supposed.

TWO...

The Interview

"The final test which comes to all
Results in changes
Rise or fall."

L Standish, 'Fortune's Corner'

THE NERVES rolling through my body was enough to make me sick. Today was interview day and although I was prepared, I wished it were just all over. I sat on the bed re-reading my application, going over my portfolio to ensure all my original qualifications were enclosed, staring blindly at the pages...

Cara had given me a good briefing on how to ready myself for today, noting that the majority of the assessments would come from the criteria I had addressed when I applied, and the interview, simply from the capabilities. I still didn't love the spotlight, didn't love public speaking, and like it or not, this was another form of it.

Lorien had thankfully given me my space this morning, letting me know that all bets were off half an hour before I had to leave for work, and here he was at the door. Time was obviously up. "Breakfast is ready Baby," he said, sitting on the bed next to me. "How are you doing?"

"I think I'm going to be sick," I laughed nervously as he took my hand.

"You'll be fine; you know the job inside-out and have been doing it long enough for them to be obviously happy with you." His warm smile gave me a shot of confidence. He was right; I knew this anyway, but it was always nice to hear it from someone else. Not that he wasn't the tiniest bit biased. "Come on," he said, standing and drawing me up to him. I got a kiss for good luck though before leaving the bedroom. How I wish I could just stay in bed with him for the rest of the day. When I posed this scenario to him, the counteroffer made it worthwhile to get in there, get it over with and get back home to him. I had no classes this afternoon; how I did love Sport day Thursday.

I toyed with the pancakes in front of me, watching my ravenous family make short work of their own pile, even Mercy. Her pancake was cut into small pieces, each one dripping heavily in Canadian maple syrup. No cheap knockoffs in this house. "You're going to rot the teeth out of her head," I said absentmindedly, taking a serviette and wiping off the slick trail from her mouth to chin.

"She'll get another set," Lorien said, leaning in to give Merce a syrupy kiss, putting the sticky goo back on her. That was not the point.

"Yuck Orrie!" she chastised and wiped the mess from her cheek with the back of her hand. I didn't have the strength to argue with her over Lorien's title this morning, and he let it slide too.

My family walked me to the door, and I smiled thinly at Lorien before bending down to give Bump a kiss goodbye. "Good luck Baby," she said and hugged my legs. I rolled my eyes at Lorien and he laughed before leaning in to kiss me.

"What time will you be home?" he asked, grabbing Mercy's bag; he was taking her to day-care.

"Usual time, around noon."

"I'll be waiting," he said and gave me a final kiss goodbye. "You'll do fine Ash, stop worrying about it." I nodded, gave Mercy a final stroke of her cheek, and left.

The morning went by so quickly, classes starting and ending before I had even realised. My mind was not on my students today though, it was on the interviews that had already started before classes commenced for the day. I had no idea how many had applied, no idea of who my competition was. It was all I could think about, and finally, my last class for the day ended and I was off to Mrs Lawper's office, as prepared as I was ever going to be.

There were three on the panel, Mrs Lawper of course, the other permanent music teacher, Andrew Dean and surprisingly, Alan O'Dowd. He greeted me with a cheery grin, and I relaxed instantly, returning the smile.

The five questions they asked me were easy enough to answer but I found myself rabbiting on and quickly pulled myself back into line. I had brought some examples of my work and they thumbed through them thoughtfully. I was hoping I was the only one to show this initiative and it would end up being my lock. The assessment tasks, of which there were two, were sent electronically to me in advance, so that part had already been completed.

And then, it was all over, and I was standing, shaking each of their hands in turn, thanking them for their time. Alan once again beamed at me, but I was unsure as to whether this was a sign of accomplishment or he was just glad to see me. I would find out soon enough. As I crossed the road toward home, I remembered Lorien's promise and found myself nearly trotting. To hell with the interview!

All was quiet when I entered the house and I called to him, "Lorien?" No answer. I ascended the stairs and found him in our room, headphones on, fingers flying across the keyboard. No wonder he hadn't heard me, and I stood, contemplating whether I should interrupt him. He stopped a few seconds later and turned to me, removing the headset. "How did you know I was here?" I asked.

"Your aroma," was his simple answer and he rose and drew me into his arms, his tongue working its way over my lips and into my mouth. "What questions did they ask you," he asked eventually, nuzzling into my neck.

"How would I describe my classroom management style," I murmured.

"Uh huh..." His hands were working on my buttons, then unhooking my bra at the rear.

"Explain how I would prepare, structure and implement a unit of work to cater to a diverse range of students." The zip of my skirt was lowered, and his fingers found the edge of my briefs, sliding them down.

"And?"

"What were the main components in achieving intended learning outcomes."

"I see..." I stepped out of my heels as Lorien slid my briefs over my feet, tossing them aside. His hot mouth worked its way up my calf as his hand slithered between my thighs, invoking a loud groan. I heard him chuckle. What was I talking about again?

"Ahhh, ummm," I was having a hard time concentrating... "Explain how I evaluate, assess and measure successful learning outcomes. And finally, something about effective communication skills." There, I was done, and I lowered my hand to his head as he began to feast.

"Let's hear it Baby, show me your effective communication skills...," he purred.

"Don't stop what you're doing," I breathed.

"You can do better than that," he instructed, and I whimpered as he snaked his tongue inside me.

"Fuck me Lorien," I begged.

"Oh Baby, that's much better," he said and stood, pulling off his shirt and shorts in two graceful movements. As our mouths fused, he backed me against the wall and lifted me onto his hips, using the wall as my support. He teased me at first, pushing in hard and drawing out completely before repeating the act.

"Please," I exhaled into his mouth, biting on his bottom lip. He took me in earnest, moving me upward with each focussed force. His hands found their way to the back of my knees, pulling me slightly lower as my back slid down the wall. He was so muscular and eventually drew us away from the wall, holding me up with his strong arms. I rode him and he stood motionless, allowing me to writhe against him, finally crying out as I found my crest. Lorien carried me to the bed, knowing I was exhausted, never breaking our connection. His grind became slow and intense, and I joined him in the final act, staring intently into each other's eyes.

"I love you so much Ashlyn," he whispered, kissing a small trail around my ear, fluttering with his tongue. He knew what this did to me.

"I love you too Lorien," I said, pressing my palms to his cheeks and moving his face so I could look into his eyes again. The kiss that ended the lovemaking went on for quite some time.

Laying there in the afterglow, I remembered to mention to Lorien about Alan. "Not surprising," he mused, "he would be the best person to be the independent." A non-involved panel member played an unbiased part in the decision making, not to mention that a female and a male also had to be present. Fairness and equity was a big thing in government positions. "Did he drop you any clues?"

"He gave me a big smile when I left, not that it necessarily means anything."

"I think so Baby, sounds like you got it."

"How can you say that, they had more interviews after me."

"I have my suspicions," he said and smiled down at me lying in his arms. "When will you find out?"

"As soon as they have made a recommendation and it goes through the approval process. It could be weeks."

"No more thinking about it, OK? It's all over now, and I *know* you will be working at Sommersett as a music teacher for as long as you want the job." I hoped he was right.

Several days came and went, and not even a whisper on the outcome of the interviews had been heard. I was starting to lose hope, and when I was called into Mrs Lawper's office the following morning, I knew my worst fears were about to be realised. "Take a seat Ashlyn," she offered, and I slumped, moreso than perched on the seat. I felt sick. She gave me a warm smile, and I appreciated her levity. "I am sorry this has taken so long for a result, but unfortunately we are not able to reveal the results until Head Office has completed the corporate side of the paperwork." She shuffled some papers in front of her, tapping them neatly into a pile before putting them on the desk next to a records management file. My Personnel record I assumed.

I was musing over her last comment, wondering if I was about to be offered the position, then telling myself not to get my hopes up, although a small gleam of anticipation had managed to work itself in. "Ashlyn?" Mrs Lawper questioned. She had been speaking to me it would seem, during my little lapse of concentration, and I was suddenly all ears again.

"I'm sorry Mrs Lawper, please continue," I responded, trying to make it seem I had been paying full attention.

"I'm waiting for your answer Ashlyn," she said, and I was unable to read the expression on her face. Oh God! If she had offered me the position, how would it look that I hadn't been listening. If she had asked me something else, yet I responded in kind to my latter scenario, I would look like an idiot. Either option I had would make me look the fool, so I had to bite the bullet and admit I had been 'otherwise' engaged.

Fortunately, Mrs Lawper smiled kindly at me before continuing. "Perhaps I should start from the beginning," she said, and smiled again. This smile held a little more of a hint of enjoyment than the previous one. I blushed, then nodded. "We have been more than happy with your performance whilst a casual teacher at this school, and you interviewed very well. Alan O'Dowd sang your praises, which was to be expected..." She paused there, and looked over her glasses at me, a twinkle of mischief in her eye. I did believe she was enjoying this immensely! I wanted to tell her to get on with it! Her teasing smile broke into a wide grin, finally saying, "We would like to offer you the permanent full-time position Ashlyn. We hope that for the benefit of Sommersett High School and its music students, that your answer will be yes."

"Yes," I blurted out, then laughed. Mrs Lawper joined me, and then stood. I stood also and took her outstretched hand, sealing the deal with a handshake.

"You will need to sign the acceptance letter which I don't have with me at present, but I have been given the authority to offer you the job. It should arrive within a few days via email directly to you. When it does, please sign, scan, and send it back to Human Resources. That will be the last of it. And, as you have already been here for some time, you will not be expected to commence on the base salary, instead continuing on from what salary grade you are currently on. I assume this is satisfactory to you?" It was most satisfactory.

Lorien took me out for dinner that night. A celebration was in order, and I was not one to refuse. Elijah happily sat with Mercy and looked after her meal and bedtime rituals, giving us the night off. "So, Mrs Standish," Lorien started, placing his fork on the table beside his empty dessert plate. "All over, red rover?" I nodded. The smile that launched itself onto my face when Mrs Lawper gave me the good news, was still etched there. Permanently it would seem.

"I'm so happy Lorien. Life is very good, and I can't imagine it being any better than this, ever!"

"Swings and roundabouts Baby, swings and roundabouts. We get the bad to appreciate the good."

"Wow you are a downer Lorien!" I exclaimed. "Are you saying bad things are just around the corner? That my little moment of sunshine will soon be overcast with clouds?" Lorien laughed, his deep chuckle resounding through the restaurant, making people turn to us and smile.

"No Ash, not at all. But how would it be if we lived in a constant state of euphoria? It would get pretty bland eventually, and we would never know the pleasure of a simple indulgence, nor a complex win. The pleasure of a kiss from a loved-one." He leant over to me, and kissed me softly. I blushed and looked around. He chuckled again, lower this time, and cupped my chin with his hand, caressing softly. "I love you so much Ashlyn," he confided in a quiet tone, his eyes bright and intense. We left shortly after.

Bing, bang, boom. We ran up to our room. Our lovemaking was powerful and urgent, then coursing down to the sweet and supple. Lorien flipped me over, putting us into the missionary position, and maintained his slow thrust, staring intently into my eyes, his fire making me burn. And then, the things that you only read about, happened. In ran Mercy, and flung herself on Lorien's back, riding him like a cowboy on a steed.

"Giddy Up Orrie!" she cawed, digging her heels into her father's ribs, holding herself upright with a handful of his 'mane'.

"Holy shit!" I shrieked, trying to get out from under Lorien. He held me motionless, saying,

"No." He was trying not to laugh, and I could not see one thing that was funny about this situation. "Let me handle this." He was calm, a true contrast to his daughter currently rounding up the cattle. She was oblivious to what was happening beneath her. How could Lorien be so unfazed by this? "Bump! Off!" he ordered in the most severe voice I think I had ever heard from him. It worked though. Mercy stopped immediately, mid-spur. She was looking down at me over her father's shoulder; a surprised face was all I could see. Now the disbelief from her dramatic entrance had waned, it was funny. But, I held my smile at bay. She back-skittered off Lorien like a crab down a rock and landed on the floor with a light thump. I could see she was confused and didn't understand why her Orrie was being so mean to her. I adjusted the covers, making sure we were both concealed before Lorien edged to the end of the bed, his feet firmly on the floor in front of hers. "You are meant to knock," he said, drawing each word out slowly to better sink into her head. "It is also nearly midnight, and you should be asleep in bed." She lowered her eyes, taking in this information and realising she had been busted. Lorien stood and flicked his robe over himself quickly, then took her by the hand, leading her back to her bedroom. "Say goodnight to your mother," he instructed, continuing the role of pissed parent.

"Night Mummy," she whispered, and gave me a small wave. She then drew the left side of her mouth in and raised an eyebrow. *Oh well* her expression seemed to say. I smiled back at her and returned her small wave. Her little toothy-pegs then glinted at me through the half-light of the darkened room. And then they were gone.

Easter School Holidays

"I'm jealous Baby.
When I see you in my arms, in the mirror's hidden charms,
The guy I'm lookin' at, steely eyes just like a cat,
Forever be my lady."

L Standish, 'Green Eyes'

MERCY WAS EXCITED. Uncle Michael was having a party today and to top it all off, it was the first day of Easter school holidays. I was pretty happy too as I had two weeks off work. "Mummy, what time are we going to Uncle Michael's?" she asked, scrambling into bed between us.

"You are supposed to knock, Mercy," Lorien reminded her, and she sighed deeply before climbing back out of bed and returning to the door. When we realised what she was doing, it was hard to keep the laughter from bubbling to the surface. *Knock knock*, she rapped twice then called, "Can I come in now?"

"Yes Bump, come on in," I answered and Lorien and I shared a smile. I turned onto my side to face my family as she tucked herself in under Lorien's awaiting raised arm. "And in answer to your question, we will be going over after lunch."

"Can we have lunch now?" She didn't understand our reaction when Lorien and I both burst out laughing at this comment.

"How about some breakfast first?" Lorien asked with a grin.

Shortly after, Mercy wriggled out from between us and clambered out of bed, trotting into the hallway. "Close the door!" Lorien called out behind her, and she came back, slamming it shut. Kids! It was not at all, or full bore!

"What are you up to?" I asked as he sidled over to me.

"What do you think I'm *up* to?" His apparent intent was pressed hard against me and I tilted my head back, allowing him to continue the coursing of soft kisses to my throat. His muted purring had played its role of foreplay however, and he slid into me seconds later without obstruction.

"What's that smell?" I asked a few minutes later, much to Lorien's amusement.

"I'm smoking Baby... Am I going too fast for you?" he asked and smirked.

"No, seriously Lorien, what's that *smell*?" I sat up and he groaned, then paused, sniffing the air.

"I don't know, but it stinks!" We both skittered out of bed and threw our robes on, heading out the door, noses in the air. The stench led us downstairs, and halfway down, I heard Elijah's door open.

"What the hell is that stink?" he asked and joined the search party.

As we hit the bottom floor the smoke alarm shrilled, and thick, black smoke was just starting to wend from the kitchen. "Mercy?" I called, worried where she could be in that mess.

"Hi Mummy!" she chirped as she popped around the dividing wall of the kitchen. "I'm making breakfast!" When I saw the state of the oven as I rounded the corner, I moaned, wondering what exactly she had used for the condiments. My guess was play doh. The twins broke into laughter and I chastised them for encouraging her.

"Stop it!" I ordered, reaching for the oven and turning it off. I grabbed a broom and rapidly waved it under the smoke alarm, trying to diffuse the smoke and silence it. "Open the sliding door and windows please," I huffed at them, then strode past, realising they hadn't moved; instead, silent tears were rolling down their faces. A confused Mercy stood aside, watching the little show. "You aren't helping!" I reminded them as I threw the sliding door open, then went to the dining area, flinging open the curtains and windows, trying to air the room out as best as possible.

Lorien had managed to find his responsibility again, taking Mercy onto his lap as Elijah opened the oven and took the stinking mess and tray onto the verandah, dumping it on the lawn to cool down. "You know better than to play with the oven!" Lorien reprimanded her. "You could have been hurt or burnt the house down!"

"But... but..." she started, the tears welling at her lids, "I was helping, Daddy." Lorien and I looked at each other in surprise. She had finally called Lorien Daddy, something we'd been waiting for, for three long years, without prompting, or her in turn wanting something. She was a smart girl our Mercy, or possibly just lucky, as her comment had certainly dampened the intensity of the situation that was rising. Regardless, she was sent to her room for an hour to 'think about what she had done'.

"You guys are too hard on her," Elijah said, emptying about a kilo of Nutri-Grain into a bowl the size of a casserole dish. I sat at the table opposite him, one eyebrow raised, just *waiting* for him to continue.

"I wouldn't go there bro," Lorien said and slid onto the seat next to me, passing me a coffee. I gave Elijah one further eyeballing before crinkling up my nose and standing.

"I can't sit in here, it still stinks," I said and went onto the verandah to sit; the twins followed.

Michael was never one to disappoint and the party was already in full swing when we arrived, or so we thought. Music was blaring from the open lounge room doorway and gyrating figures faded into the half-shadow within. I should have known better though, it was only Michael and Glen. Mercy ran ahead to join them and broke into a rather impressive 'Running Man' for a three year old. Uncles Michael and Glen had of course taught her all the cool moves. She couldn't wait until she was old enough to go to the gay club in Castlebrook with them.

Elijah took our bags upstairs and I stood there, Lorien holding me to him from behind, watching the three children ham it up. He swayed me slightly to the rhythm, his smiling lips at my neck. It was only when the song ended that the boys came to say their hellos. Mercy got the first one of course, leaping into Michael's arms as he covered her plump cheeks with kisses. The hellos taken care of, Lorien and I were bustled out the back door to the patio.

Voices came from the deck above and I realised that we weren't the first ones here. Our voices must have also carried, as a few seconds later, trundling feet stomped their way down the stairs from above and three faces peered at us from the pool level. "Well hi!" the first male said, supporting his body weight by holding onto the deck edge above. He must have been just out of the pool as his brown body shimmered in the sunlight, a few trickles of water still running from his hair. Noticing my glance, he shook his head, covering his mates in the droplets. He was young, tanned and very good-looking. I assumed he was a friend of Michael and Glen's from Sniper's, hence the outstanding male attributes.

"Geez, thanks mate!" male number two answered, before dropping over the ledge and landing near where Lorien was standing. There was no need to take the stairs when young, or male, or having no need for them... He stuck out his hand and Lorien shook it. "Ed." He then pointed to the blonde guy, "Craig," and then the brunette bronzed Aussie, "Brett." Brunette, bronzed Brett. I chuckled to myself, then stood to shake each of their hands in turn. Triple B held it a little longer than necessary, but I didn't think too much of it. Many gay males had no issue with personal space, especially friends of Michael and Glen's.

Elijah walked through the door with a tray of snacks as Lorien finished the hand-shaking procession, taking a seat next to me. "These are the famous Standish twins," Michael remarked, following Elijah out the door with more trays of food. Elijah rolled his eyes at Michael, before smiling at the three newcomers to our brood, once again shaking hands.

"And what am I?" Mercy chirped behind him. "Chopped liver?" Where the hell did she learn this stuff? My guess was Uncle Michael, and he confirmed this by laughing loudly before swinging her back into his arms.

"And these two," Michael said, gesturing to me and planting a kiss on Mercy's cheek, "are the famous Standish women." Mercy beamed at him, and I, like Elijah, simply rolled my eyes at him.

"I want to swim!" Mercy informed Uncle Michael.

"Soon Bump."

"No! Now! Where's Aunty Bree and Uncle Simon?" she demanded.

"Mercy!" Lorien warned, then added, "Your Aunt and Uncle are not here today." He then leant over to me. "Want to come in with us Mummy? Give Uncle Michael a little break?" I smiled at him and nodded, standing, and dropped my shorts on the chair. Lorien scooped up the towels and threw Mercy over his shoulder on his way past Michael, and I trotted behind them.

I entered the pool in my usual coy fashion, letting myself adjust to the water temperature before diving into the crystal depths. Lorien and Mercy were already soaked. "Swim to Mum," Lorien instructed and she doggy-paddled her way over. A few minutes later, Brett was perched on the edge of the pool, watching.

"How old?" he asked me.

"She turned three last December."

"Cute. She looks like you."

"Well thanks," I replied and smiled at our girl in my arms. She grinned back at me before splashing off toward her father. Lorien and I both knew whom she most resembled, and it sure wasn't me. Well, maybe she had a smidge of my temperament. Just a little...

By 6.00 pm, I had Mercy in her PJs and ready to eat. Michael had arranged her in the upstairs spare room tonight on a single mattress on the floor. He'd also thoughtfully moved the portable TV and DVD player in too so she would doze off. Lorien and I were also in that room, and there would be no fooling around tonight. I wondered whether he had considered that already. His libido didn't usually think that far ahead so I assumed he would be in for a disappointment when 'lights out' finally arrived. Again, I chuckled to myself. I was having a really good time and the few beers hadn't hurt. I led Mercy into the kitchen, where Uncle Glen was waiting for her.

"OK, what's it to be?' he asked her.

"Chicken sandwich."

"Mercy," I interrupted before Glen had the chance, "Uncle Glen has cooked barbeque; I don't think a chicken sandwich is on the menu."

"But I don't feel like snags or rissoles, I feel like chicken." She climbed down off the stool and started to make her way out the back.

"Where are you going?" I asked, hands on hips.

"To get Daddy; he will go and buy me chicken." Glen had been reaching into the fridge during this interlude and pulled out a container, and thankfully, a shredded barbecue chicken was inside.

"Daddy?" he whispered as he started on buttering the bread, carefully removing the crusts. He knew Mercy's eating habits, and was also aware that she had never called Lorien Daddy.

"Started today," I answered softly. He raised his eyebrows and smiled, nodding. Mercy hadn't realised that her chicken-wish was about to be realised, so I took her by the shoulders and directed her back to the stool.

"Ohh! *Thank* you, Uncle Glen."

When Mercy was happily munching away, I asked Glen about Brett, Ed and Craig. "They're patrons of the club?"

"No," he laughed, "they are straight guys. Brett does Sniper's books and Ed and Craig are his mates." I was a little surprised to hear this; Simon was our friendly neighbourhood accountant.

"Why doesn't Simon do your accounting?"

"Too close to home, he reckons," Glen responded. "He prefers a professional relationship with his clients." I was glad Simon still did our taxes, but I suppose a long-term friendship was a little different to doing accounting for an entire business.

I felt hands slip over my shoulders, and I turned to kiss a waiting Lorien. "Is she nearly ready for a movie?" he asked.

"Hmmp," Mercy responded.

"Was that a yes?" And she nodded at her father, confirming this.

"Anything in particular?" She swallowed this time, before answering.

"Charlie." Charlie referred to 'Charlie and the Chocolate Factory', or at times possibly 'Willy Wonka and the Chocolate Factory'. She swapped between the two, and although both old movies, she loved them. I think any three year old would love to be trapped in a factory of chocolate. I know I adored the Charlie story when I was growing up. It was the more recent version she was craving tonight, however.

When she was settled, we both kissed her goodnight and told her we'd be back to check on her soon. Unkie Lie stuck his head through the door leading to the top deck to say his goodnights also. "Get off my bed Lori," he said to his twin, who was currently sprawled over it, hands linked behind his head. Lorien smiled and sat upright, moving to the edge.

"I thought we were sleeping in here," I said, looking to Lorien.

"Not tonight," he answered.

"Pre-arranged?" I countered, now looking at Elijah with one eyebrow raised.

"Of course, Ash. You don't think he'd be going without tonight, do you?" he asked sarcastically.

"God, Lorien," I tsked.

"You can say that later Baby, call it out in fact." I shook my head and led them out the sliding door to the deck, blowing Bump a kiss on the way. She caught it in her hand and smacked it to her cheek, returning the gesture three times to each of us. I did enjoy our family night-time rituals, including calling out 'God, Lorien' if I were to be honest.

We Indian-filed down the two sets of stairs to join the party on the lower level; a few more people had arrived. I took my original place next to Lorien and were introduced to the newcomers, then waited on Elijah to return from the drinks run. He handed us a beer a few minutes later and took a seat next to one of the newly arrived, Deb. Lorien jabbed me in the ribs with his elbow and I responded by telling him to grow up. Like that was *ever* going to happen!

I felt a tap on my arm and turned to see Brett had sat down, wanting to start a conversation. Now I knew he wasn't gay, I was a little more guarded in my reactions to him. It was easy to flirt with a gay man, knowing that nothing would come of it; it was a completely different situation when a straight man though, despite the trio of 'off-the-market' rings that adorned my left ring finger. "So, Brett, you know the guys through Snipers," I said.

"Yes, I do their books."

"Glen was telling me."

"I'm not gay though." I had to laugh at that.

"That doesn't worry any of us; we grew up with Michael." Hearing his name, Michael looked across the table and tilted his head to the side, questioning why his name had been brought up. I shook my head, letting him know it wasn't important. Regardless, he trotted over and sat between Brett and me, perched on the brick retaining wall.

"Grew up with Michael?" he continued for us.

"I was just telling Brett that his being, or not being gay, is not an issue as we had grown up with you."

"Ahhh, always such an important part of the conversation." I wasn't sure what he meant, and acknowledging the confusion on my face, continued. "You know, Michael this and Michael that; Michael is fabulous, Michael, Michael, Michael…"

"Oh, how stupid of me," I said and waved my hand in a regal gesture, bowing as deeply to him as my sitting position would allow. "Sir Michael…"

"That's better," he quipped and laughed, running his hand over my back. "Although," he added mischievously, "I would love to try and turn this one," he said, smiling cheekily at Brett.

"Oi!" Glen called out from the other side of the table.

"Oh precious!" Michael exclaimed, "You know there is no other than you!" He skittered back over to Glen and embraced him from behind, crossing his arms over Glen's chest and kissing at his neck. I think he was forgiven.

"How long have you known them?" Brett asked, gesturing toward Michael and Glen with his chin.

"Michael... since Year 7 and Glen we met a few years ago."

"I have only known Michael for eight years though, Eli and I weren't part of the original Sommersett mob," Lorien interjected.

"So, you're an original hey?" Brett lobbed back at me, smirking.

"I suppose so."

"She's one of a kind," Lorien added, drawing me to him for a kiss. When the forehead magnets allowed us to part, Brett had gone.

As the night went on, the music grew louder and the amber fluid poured more rapidly. The jokes also became bawdier. I was sitting on Lorien's knee chatting to Deb whilst the twins exchanged conversation, when Brett approached me, holding out his hands. I think he wanted me to dance with him. Lorien absentmindedly raised his hands from my hips to let me up, but I didn't want to. I had noticed Brett watching me throughout the night. A few glances over my shoulder confirmed this, as no one or nothing spectacular was behind me. His gaze was creepy and reminiscent of Matty, the drummer in our defunct band 'Listening at Keyholes'. The thought made me shudder. This was a character trait I did not want to engage with again!

Brett moved forward, seeing he had Lorien's approval, and I sat further back into Lorien's lap, shaking my head at Brett. "I'm fine where I am," I told him.

"Nah," he slurred, being one of the partakers of the rapid-pouring amber fluid. He grabbed both of my wrists, trying to pull me to my feet. He swayed and eddied, making it seem his own feet were on a sailboat deck, in heavy seas. The spittle from his mouth even provided the ocean spray as he slurred again, "Stand up." I felt Lorien tighten his arms around me and try to stand simultaneously, both protective and defensive at the same time. I turned to face him and smiled, as his actions had counteracted themselves. It was funny, and although gross, I felt in no danger from Brett's drunken actions. I had my Lorien's arms around me.

It was not Lorien though who ended up reacting, to put an end to this. I saw two hands come from behind Brett, pulling him roughly by the shoulders. This did not help however, as Brett still had me by the wrists. As a result, I was yanked forward, and I twisted my hands in an attempt to loosen his grasp. "Eli!" I heard Lorien call. "Stop it, you're pulling Ash with him!" It all happened so fast and as Brett stumbled and fell sideways, finally letting me go, I reached my 'no return' point and tumbled off Lorien's lap, face down onto the pavers. Thankfully, Mercy was in bed!

Lorien and Deb helped me to my feet, and I was undamaged. My hands, which caught my fall had a few small rocks pressed into them, which I brushed off on my jeans. Lorien started to fuss, which I quickly put an end to, more interested in getting over to Elijah to stop what was occurring before me.

As Brett tried to get to his feet, Elijah pushed his foot into the small of Brett's back, pinning him to the ground. "Stop it Elijah!" I said, taking his arm and trying to move him away. Brett was an idiot, but didn't need this kind of treatment, and I was OK. It was nothing worse than what could happen at a club or pub. We were also all friends of Michael and Glen's and that meant a little leniency, surely. Elijah did not stop.

"That's enough," said the calming Lorien, now at his twin's side. "I think he's got the point." Elijah stopped the foot work, and stood, just staring down at Brett as he slowly made his way back to his feet.

"Cockhead," Elijah said to Brett, before heading inside. I went to follow, but Lorien stopped me.

"Let him go Ash, he needs to cool off." So I did. I wasn't sure why Elijah had reacted so badly in the first place though. He sure was pissed off!

Brett remained sheepish for the rest of the evening, finally curling up on the sofa inside, where we could hear him snoring from outside. Elijah had remained somewhat sheepish as well, and didn't get back into the swing of the party. He was currently sitting at the back of our loose circle, beer bottle clutched loosely between both hands, his elbows on his knees, eyes downcast. I went to him.

"My hero," I said and smiled, leaning up against the retaining wall near him. His reply was a snort, but he did look up, sat back and gave me half a smile.

"Sorry Ash."

"It's OK Elijah. I know you were only looking out for me."

"Yeah." He took a swig from the bottle and gave me a blank look.

"You OK?" I asked.

"Yeah," he echoed.

"Coming back to the party?"

"Yeah," he confirmed one last time, although in a brighter tone.

When I re-joined Lorien, he whispered in my ear, "He's embarrassed Ash, let it go."

"But why did he do it and why be embarrassed about it?" I asked in all curiosity.

"We're a pretty tight group Baby. It's like a pack mentality, you know. One for all, and all that." Yes, I understood what he was getting at.

Michael and Glen had been rather quiet considering what had gone down tonight. Even with Brett asleep, they did not form their usual attack when the coast was clear. Especially Michael! When I asked him about it, he didn't seem to think it was that big of a deal. Sometimes, very rarely, but sometimes, I could not work Michael out. I'd assume how he'd react to things, but he was not always steadfast to his nature. Go Michael, I supposed!

Music Theory

"She doesn't always know it
But the beauty of her face,
Keeps my heart racing faster
As does the music of her grace."

L Standish, 'Standing in Her Shadow'

THE FINAL DRESS REHEARSAL was in full swing. The hours of
practise, at school and in their own bedrooms, much to their family's
dismay no doubt, had paid off. The kids were ready for show time. "OK,
you guys are ready!" I called in excitement, fist pumping my left hand in
the air and feeling a little ridiculous in doing so. It was met with a
resounding cheer of triumph. "But..." I started, and a collective groan now
echoed through the ensemble. "Wait a minute; this is just a couple of
reminders, and to you all. Firstly cast, slow down! We finished this last
rehearsal ten minutes before schedule. You need to stop racing through
the scenes and songs." They looked around at each other, a few
awkward grins shone out, and more than one set of hands went to their
mouths to stifle a giggle. Yes, they knew. We had discussed this many
times before. "When you speed up, the band speeds up, then everyone
speeds up! Band," I said, now looking toward them, "YOU need to keep
the pace. Don't take off the second one of the cast starts racing for the
finish line." It was now the band's turn to smile and giggle. They also
knew this. My finger pointed with intent at the drummer especially. "You
are in charge Mark, keep them on track!" He smiled and dropped his gaze

to his sticks, twirling the right one between his fingers before rattling off a Bah Dum Bum – denoting a punchline, but this was far from a joke.

The band was an odd assortment of instruments. If you played an instrument, you were in the show, like it or not. The show band consisted of two clarinets, a saxophone, oboe, tenor horn, keyboard, drums, and base and lead guitars. The other musicians were currently on stage – no playing of an instrument for them tonight. I had no idea how difficult it was to write an oboe into a music composition so it would merge with the other timbres. The oboe was such a sad and mournful sounding woodwind, and was more at home in an orchestra than a high school rock show. However, I had prevailed! No help from Lorien either.

The multi-purpose centre had been set up with rows of chairs, filling the entire space other than the first few metres directly in front of the stage, set aside for the band, and an aisle down the middle of the room. The students were excited and chatty, making it a difficult task to have them follow instruction, or even take notice. The show wasn't due to start for another two hours, but we had all reassembled at 5 pm to start on make-up and last-minute costume ironing, after an early dinner of sausage sandwiches cooked on the school barbecue. Lorien and Elijah would arrive nearer the start time, leading a fed, and hopefully bathed, Mercy. I could not have managed the horde of students plus Lorien so close to show time, so instructed him to stay home until at least 6.30 pm. He would have been a massive help, I know, but would have also been a massive hindrance. I needed a clear head and thinking space.

Even though this was an annual event, as was the combined Hunter-wide schools' Starstruck concert, this was the function I preferred. I assumed this was because it was a one-off performance, and did not require numerous off-site rehearsals and actual shows. It was the matinees for Starstruck that was the killer. Keeping the kids entertained for hours between afternoon and evening shows, plus knowing their whereabouts, was like catching rainwater in a sieve. "Mrs Standish!" I heard called. I turned to find a near-weeping Sophie; her costume clutched in her hands. A small string of sequin ribbon had come away from her skirt hem, and I took it from her, placing a calming hand on her back.

"Easily fixed!" I confirmed and headed for the backstage dressing-room area, which I had equipped for such emergencies. Scissors, varying colours of thread, glue, buttons, zippers, hook and eyes, press studs, 1,000 or so needles, you name it. I had it. I quickly stitched the ribbon into place, snapping off the thread with my teeth, as I handed it back to Sophie. She smiled at me in thanks, and I headed off to deal with the next emergency I saw developing.

"What!?" I asked the two boys, playing tug-o-war with a pair of black pants, bearing the same black sequin ribbon down the sides of the seam. I could see I would be fixing those as well if I didn't put a stop to it immediately. "Give me those!" I said, and took the offending garment from an unwilling pair of hands.

"These are mine!" James admonished, throwing a dirty look in Will's direction, and attempting to reclaim them from me.

"No, mine! Those are yours!" Will answered, his head gesturing to another pair on the floor near us. He also attempted to take the pants from my hand. I yanked my hands backwards, taking the pants with me, escaping from both of their eager clutches.

"First of all," I started, "What is a pair doing on the floor anyway? You have all been told to look after your costumes as they are the only set!" The textiles students had been busy designing and crafting these costumes for several weeks and it had saved a lot of money. Neither boys had an answer and I stooped to pick the homeless pair from the floor. I looked inside both waistbands and saw they were the exact same size. My hands dropped to my sides, one pair in each and looked at the boys with a 'you're kidding me' expression on my face. "Does it matter?"

"Mine were ironed!" Will explained, a little more dramatically than needed.

"No, mine!" challenged James. They both came at the pants again.

"I will iron them both, as they both now need it, don't they?" I pointed out, and headed once again into the dressing-room.

Lorien's head popped through the open door. "Hey Baby!" he called, leading Mercy in by the hand.

"Lorien! The girls could have been dressing!" I accused.

"You're in the boy's dressing-room," he reminded me with a grin.

"Well, what about Mercy?"

"Door was open," he said and shrugged. He knew the rules as well as anyone. Open door meant OK to enter. Still… And then I realised…

"It's 6.30!" I nearly shrilled.

"On the dot," he said smugly, as I took Mercy in my arms for a hug to calm me down.

"You look funny Mummy," she told me, arching back a little to look at my face.

"I'm a little stressed Merce," was the only explanation I could give as I handed her back to Lorien. I cocked one half of my mouth up in a half smile and rolled my eyes at him.

"Come on Mercy, let's leave Mum to it. She is very busy." He leant forward and kissed me gently. This was met with a few catcalls and good-natured whistles from the boys. I blushed, then shooed Lorien from the room.

"Are you all ready?" I asked, ignoring their jibes.

"Yes Mrs Standish," they chorused in a robotic voice. I shook my head and took the corridor behind the stage that led to the girl's dressing-room to give the girls a final hurry-up.

Seriously! 10 metres of corridor, and what do I find. Two seniors, tongue jousting in its shadowy seclusion. I clapped my hands together, as if ready for a game of slaps, and guided their interlocked force between their chests, breaking them apart. "You, go!" I instructed Colin, pointing to the boys' dressing-room, "And, you, come!" I told Kate, bustling her in front of me toward the girls'. The chatter and excitement coming from the girl's side was a cacophony compared to the boys'. The air was pungent with perfume and hairspray and the counters littered in little tubes, bottles and eye-colour palettes. All the china-painted dolls scattered around the room and seated at the make-up counters were creating an orchestra of their own. Cheeks were heavily rouged, eyes glimmered with the intensity of the sparkled makeup, lips glistened red, and hair shone. As I was admiring the girls, looking absolutely stunning, a rather irritated Andi approached me through the crowd.

"Miss! We can't stretch in here, it's too packed!" she called above the ruckus. Andi was one of the lead dancers, and their pre-warmups had not taken place yet due to the lack of space. I wondered vaguely where Karen Smith was. Not that it mattered; this was an issue of space, not dance instruction.

"Go up on stage then, and keep it quiet!" I called back. Andi and the rest of the dance troupe took to the stage, bouncing nimbly up the three stairs that led there, disappearing into the blackness. I checked my watch, and it was five to seven. I bolted out to the band and got their attention. The keyboard struck middle C, and the rest of the members came in on their correct note, ensuring they were all in tune. I then mentally ticked off a list in my head. Had I covered everyone?

With the band tuning up, the crowd began to settle. This was always a signal that the show was about to start. I glanced around to see how many seats we had filled, and the kids had done me proud. There was not a vacant chair to be seen. I caught Lorien's wave and saw him sitting with my parents, Mercy, Elijah, our friends and Mrs Lawper. Mum had Mercy on her knee and was involved in an in-depth conversation with the Headmistress. Her hand gestured to the right of the stage at the piano sitting there on the floor, and Mum nodded. I found it odd as the piano did not play a part in tonight's performance. That same piano Lorien and I had made love on, not too long ago... I shuddered at the thought, totally inappropriate for tonight's performance, and turned back to the band. I quickly stuck my head through the curtain and the cast, assembled on both sides of the stage, gave me the thumbs up. We were ready.

My immediate job for the night was to conduct the band. They would stay together and in time tonight if it killed me. I raised my baton, also a signal for Andrew Dean to raise the curtain, and the show burst into life.

The first Act went smoothly, with only one hiccup when Coral had a small skid as she exited the stage at the end of one of the songs, but hardly noticeable. My head was pounding. Trying to keep one eye on the band, and the other eye on the stage, was not an easy feat. Andrew, now on the smoke machine wasn't helping my thumping temples, nor Janet Kowalenko on the lights. But, all the cues took place as scheduled, including the shuffling on and off of the sets and the kids were doing a marvelous job. Suddenly, it was intermission!

I glanced at my watch. No, we had not raced through it, we were perfectly on time. The action was so fast paced it had simply dissolved the time it took to accomplish it. We had twenty minutes for costume and scenery changes, but first I wanted to find my family and friends.

I met them at the rear of the auditorium, near the food service window. Another little money saver; the food tech students had prepared all the things for sale tonight, to both eat and drink. Lorien hugged me as he handed me a watery Fruit Cup cordial, and I was amassed by hugging arms and too many voices. I was a bit flighty and after a quick hello, moved away from them, with Lorien joining me in the corner with our girl. Our girl was currently shoving in as much popcorn as her rosebud mouth would allow, waving a little friend over as she munched. I remembered him from her party, but his name escaped me.

They happily entertained themselves and I turned to Lorien, taking him in my embrace. I lay my head on his shoulder. "Rub my temples for me Lorien," I asked. He smiled down at me and reached into his pocket. First he pulled out some Panadol, which I took eagerly, and then a hip flask, which he shook at me wickedly. This I did not take eagerly. "No, Lorien, I can't!" I exclaimed and pulled away from him, laughing.

"I think you should!" he asserted, and twisted open the cap. I didn't think about it, just took his advice, took it from him, and gulped. It burnt my throat fiercely as the fluid made its way down my throat, but it felt good. It felt cleansing. I exhaled and let out a push of air. "Wooo!" Lorien laughed and reassembled the flask, pocketing it again, out of sight.

"I have to get out the back," I told him, hugging him to me one last time.

I spotted a few of the cast on the way to the dressing-rooms, directing them back as well. They were to stay in the dressing-rooms, and not be seen wandering through the audience members. I knew it was a hard instruction to follow, so proud of their achievements so far and wanting to share it with their families, but that was for the end of the show.

I checked on the boys first. Their door was already open. Everyone was changed into the next costumes and were ready to go. We still had ten minutes. "Great job guys!" I told them, and they took the praise with gentle humility. "Ready for Act 2?" They nodded in unison and fidgeted around, not sure what to do with themselves until then. I smiled and nodded, letting them know I'd see them soon from the band floor.

The girl's door was still closed. I took that time to seek out Andrew, who I found enjoying a meat pie with sauce, sitting on the top step of the stage entrance. He spotted me coming, and stood, smiling. "Show's going great!" he said, through a mouthful of meat pie.

"I know, the kids are doing a fabulous job!" He nodded and wiped at his mouth with the back of his hand, and swallowed. "As are you all," I confirmed. I had laid the bait, now time to reel in the fish. "Would you mind though, if you went a little easier on the smoke?" It's making it hard for the band kids to see their sheet music. I'm also a bit worried it might be affecting the voices of the cast that have to sing." I smiled to lighten the request.

"Sure thing Ashlyn," he said. "No problem!" I thanked him and headed off to the girl's dressing-room again. The door was open this time.

"Well done ladies!" I exclaimed as I entered the room, clapping them loudly. 'You're simply captivating!" I met Coral's eye and she went to tear-up, ashamed for her little lapse. "Now, Coral, none of that!" I said, stopping her before she could speak. First of all, no one even noticed. I was talking to Mr Standish at intermission, and he didn't even know it happened," I lied. I had not spoken to Lorien about it, but he also never mentioned it, so maybe no one did notice. It didn't matter anyway. We were at Sommersett High School, not Broadway. "And secondly", I continued, "you will ruin your makeup!" I put one palm on her cheek, wiping away the single tear that had formed. She smiled up at me, and nodded, wrapping her arms around my waist. After a brief hug, she headed back to the make-up counter, and reapplied some blush. The makeup was gaudy when up close to the cast, but it had to be. Normal application wouldn't show to the audience, so the heavy-handed treatment was definitely required. I felt hands then slip around me again, but from behind this time.

"Good luck Baby, see you on the other side," Lorien said and spun me to face him. He kissed me, parted lips, but no tongue. He considered this to be OK in front of students. I did not, and drew gently away.

"Thank you my Darling," I responded quietly, kissing him again, but a peck on the lips only. He traced a finger lightly down the frame of my face, winked, and left.

As I turned, the mood in the girl's room was far different to that of the boys when Lorien had kissed me. They sat there, silent for once, mouths agape and cheeks already flushed, were now even moreso. I understood their expression. Ahhh, Mr Standish, that Knight in shining armour... Their blossoming youth now turning into the wonderment of adolescence, and with it came the unknown answer to their yearning and desires. "There are plenty of decent ones out there ladies," I confirmed. "Just wait until you get a good one!" Their mouths snapped shut and they quickly returned to whatever they had been doing, and I slipped away, retaking my place at the front of the band.

The second Act went even more smoothly than the first, and with a final fanfare from the band, the show ended. I turned to clap the cast with the rest of the audience, as the band started up once again. The lesser players retook the stage, mainly those on costumes, scenery, and food, then the minor ensemble, working through to the leads. All of them took their praise, bowing in turn, and then they all turned to the band and applauded their efforts as well. Andrew was suddenly beside me, taking me by the hand. "What...?" I muttered, confused as to where he was leading me. And right onto the stage is where I ended up.

The crowd was already on their feet before I came on stage, but the applause intensified on my arrival. I heard a few whistles, and knew they came from Lorien and/or Michael. I couldn't hide my smile, nor my blush and I started to cry when the two leads handed me a bunch of roses. They stepped back and continued with the applause. Mrs Lawper then approached from the stage-left steps, a microphone in her hand.

The noise settled and the band struck out the last few notes of the hit song that had been playing throughout the applause, and the tick of the microphone as Mrs Lawper turned it on, could be heard. "Thank you Mrs Standish for a smashing version of this show!" The applause started again, and died down when Mrs Lawper drew her arms out, signaling for silence. "And to the amazing cast, band and all those who helped behind the scenes!" The applause thundered once more. After a few minutes, Mrs Lawper again asked for shush.

The kids started to leave the stage as Mrs Lawper made a few announcements whilst she had the parents all together, including what we had raised tonight, and I likewise, wanted to make my escape. Andrew held fast onto me though. Again, I muttered, "What...?" I was now even more confused. He just smiled at me and patted my arm. A chair was thrust against me from behind, forcing me into it, raising a titter from the audience, and I felt the bouquet being lifted from my arms. I looked around bewildered, not knowing what was going on. Andrew and Mrs Lawper then exited the stage and the lights went off. Seconds later, a soft spotlight appeared over the piano, and I saw my Lorien seated there, ready to play. *Play what?* Again, my mind tried to fathom the goings-on.

The auditorium was in complete darkness, with the exception of Lorien and the piano, and I heard Mrs Lawper, through the microphone say, "And now presenting Mr Lorien Standish, giving us an abridged version of his new rock opera, which will be an outstanding success. For those of you who do not know, both Lorien and Ashlyn attended Sommersett High School and found their love of music and each other, whilst here. We are so proud of them both and what they have achieved in their lives, and hope that a little bit of Sommersett High School had something to do with it. Mr Standish, if you please..." Mrs Lawper finished.

Lorien looked in my general direction and winked, then threw his hands into the air, bringing them down with tremendous force, playing out three quick chords that seemed to hang in the air. He then played like I had never heard him play before. I was mesmerized, and thankful that I was sitting in the dark. No one could see the tears streaming down my face as my hands clutched at my skirt, caught up in the extravaganza unfolding before me.

The band accompanied him after five minutes and backed him perfectly, adding the flourishing touches that the piano alone could not portray. In the dim half-light I could see the other music students who had been in the cast had now joined the band or formed the choir, adding to the depth and sweetness of the music. My clever students and my clever husband, not to mention clever Mrs Lawper, contrived this without my knowledge. My heart swelled again with the love I had for Lorien, and my life as a total full circle. With the exception of my wedding day and the birth of our Mercy, I had never felt so alive, so loved and so complete. My life was a miracle, and I was so thankful for everything it contained.

As the last bass note resonated into silence, the crowd was again on its feet, deafening in the intensity. The lights blinked on and I realised I had stood, and was walking toward Lorien, hardly able to see through the shimmer of gauze my tears had formed over my vision. He lifted me from the stage and swung me around, whispering to me, "You liked it?"

"Oh Lorien!" I cried. "There are no words to describe how amazing that was, how amazing you are. I love you so much!" and then our lips met, and I could hear the crowd no longer.

After I had pulled myself together, we headed to the rear of the auditorium again, this time for coffee and cake. Lorien and I chatted to students, parents, faculty and friends, sometimes as a single unit, and sometimes as a couple. Everyone was on such a high and I couldn't wait to get home to prove the strength of my love to my husband. I was *so* horny! I looked around for Mercy and saw her again with her friend. I also took notice of the conversation they were having. It grabbed both of our attention, as it had become a little heated. "I am too going to marry my Daddy!" Mercy exclaimed, hands on hips.

"Girls can't marry their Dads!" Her friend replied, hands also rising to settle on his own hips. I believed this was blanket-boy, aka Noah. And Noah had seemed to have found his strength. Perhaps a little of Mercy had rubbed off on him.

"Oh yeah!" she challenged. "Why not? My Mummy did!" It would appear the argument had been settled. There was no retort to that logic, and none was heard.

"Mummy and Daddy seem to be locked in now, hey?" Lorien said. I smiled up at him, expressing my joy at her words through the smile on my face and the glisten in my eyes.

"Come on, let's go," I said and herded he and Mercy outside.

"Wow, I love this version of Ashlyn," Lorien murmured, the heat in his eyes matching my force as I pushed him roughly onto the bed about three minutes after we walked through the door. Elijah was in charge of putting Mercy to bed and I had dragged Lorien up the stairs.

I yanked at his pants before Lorien helped by undoing the button and zip and he sprung up at me, ready for action. "See the affect you have on me Baby," he crooned, reaching for me. I had my clothes pooled around my feet in seconds, then fell on him like a starving vampire about to feed. For once, I solely led this dance, and Lorien was happy for me to take the control. I glided myself over him, parting my eager lips to tease him, not allowing him to penetrate me just yet. He snickered, trying to manoeuvre me into place so he could thrust into me from below, but I wouldn't let him.

"Something funny?" I asked, sidling up his body, ending with my straddle across his throat.

"Nuh uh," he said, drawing me forward, aligning me to his waiting mouth. I leant back slightly, moaning, taking his searching tongue deeper within my confines. He lapped and brought his fingers up to separate me further, forcing my sensitive nerve to react immediately to his force. I rode him, allowing every cell in my body to respond to this elevated plain, as Lorien clutched at my thighs, his fingers still probing me open to him. As I eased, I lowered my forehead to rest on his own, lightly kissing the tip of his nose, eyelids and each cheek.

"I love you Lorien," I breathed. And his retort, my favourite words from him, softly whispered,

"Show me how you love me..."

ONE...

Lorien

"And if I knew my last words to you
Would haunt us both forever
I'd change the sin and call the wind
To hold you soft, like fine leather."

L Standish, 'Butterfly Storm'

I SIDLED OUT OF BED slowly, to not wake Ash. I wanted to get into Rondo and back before she woke if possible. I had commissioned a special necklace for her, a small ying-yang pendant made up of diamonds and onyx. It was identical to the one I had bought her for our first Valentine's Day together, although this one being more ornate.

I dressed quickly, then went to wake Mercy. I was going to drop her off at Anna and Dom's on the way. We would also eat breakfast there. Ashlyn deserved a sleep-in, as did Elijah. "Merce," I whispered through the crack in Elijah's door. For once it appeared she had stayed in her own bed as the dawn came creeping through her window. I then remembered Elijah was already at the hospital, filling his Emergency Room requirements. I opened her door slowly and peeked in. Yes, she was still asleep.

I crawled in next to her and she snuggled into me. "Daddy?" she asked sleepily, her sweet breath tickling at my fringe. She had called me Daddy again. This was a name I never tired of hearing, now she had finally given up on 'Orrie'.

"Yes Bump, are you ready to get up? We're going to Grandma and Grandpa's this morning." She mumbled something incoherent, and I held her for a few minutes more, adoring her, loving her.

Mercy loved being on the bike. I helped her put her helmet, jacket and gloves on, and then I climbed on, hoisting her up in front of me. She knew to hold on tight and keep still. There were rules on this bike, and if she didn't obey them, there would be no more bike rides. It still freaked her mother out when Mercy rode with me, so, more often than not, we would sneak away like thieves in the night. Well, in the morning, as was the case today. It was also illegal for a child under 7 to ride pillion, but we only ever did local jaunts, and she did love it so.

"Wheeeeeeeeeeeeee!" sang out Mercy's little chirp as I kicked it into gear and sped from the house. It would have woken Ashlyn I am sure, and she would have heard Mercy's excited squeal. It was also tradition now, that little 'Whee'. I think the first time Mercy came with me, there was more than a little wee running down Ash's leg. The memory made me smile.

There was little traffic on the road at this time of the morning, and we were in Warden in less than ten minutes. Mercy didn't want to get off the bike. "More Daddy, more!"

"I will be back soon, and then you will get to ride home with me. OK?" She nodded in agreement and I left shortly thereafter.

The best part of riding a motorbike, well other than the freedom, speed and ability to move with abandon, was the ease of parking. I pulled up outside the Rondo manufacturing jewellers and goose-stepped the bike backwards to the kerb, turning off the ignition. I removed my helmet before entering the shop, not wanting them to think I was about to rob them.

The woman behind the counter met me with a welcoming smile. She knew me by sight, and why I had commissioned this piece, giving her the cheaper original to copy. She obviously got a great deal of joy from her job, knowing she was making couples happy. And the jeweller had not disappointed me.

She laid the pendant on a piece of black velvet, which highlighted the gemstones and onyx beautifully. It glistened and winked under the incandescent lights, inviting my hand to stroke it lightly. Ash would love it. "Is this what you were after, Mr Standish?" she asked, and once again, a smile lit up her doughy, middle-aged face.

"Yes, it is perfect."

"Any special occasion?"

"Just reminding my wife of how much she means to me." I actually believe the woman blushed. Such a romantic.

"Shall I wrap it?"

"No, I'll put it in my pocket. I'd like her to find it there," I added, tipping her a wink. She blushed again, making me laugh.

I handed over the cash and put the pendant, with a newly purchased chain to secure it, in my pocket. Thanking her again, I headed for the door, pulling my helmet on. I checked my watch as I gunned the engine; I had only been gone for an hour. By the time I picked up Mercy, we would be home by 10.00 am. Ash should be up by now, probably wondering where her little family had gone, assuming she had not heard our roaring departure. She would find out soon enough.

As the rain started, I mentally cursed myself for not bringing my wet weather gear. Mercy had a set at Anna and Dom's at least, so she would stay dry for the quick trip from Warden to Sommersett. I pulled the collar of my jacket up a little higher and hunkered into the seat. Contrary to people's beliefs, leather was not waterproof, nor was the seat, which was rapidly moistening below me. To enforce this further, the rain started to bucket down. Great.

I decided not to brave the weather like a hero, especially without my wet weather gear with the high-vis strips for better visibility to motorists. I glanced around looking for an awning, then spotted the café on the other side of the street. That would do, and a cup of coffee would warm me for the ride home when the rain started to ease. I pulled off my helmet and put it into the top box, then reached into my pocket, reclaiming the pendant, and held it in my hand. It warmed me better than any cup of coffee could do. I felt the smile at my lips as I threaded the thin chain through my fingers, stroking my thumb over the gemstones and onyx. I had slowly made my way the few metres to the pedestrian crossing during my inspection, and stepped off the curb, still marvelling at my new purchase. *Ashlyn will love this…* was my last cohesive thought.

I was unaware of the car until a flash of grey barrelled down at me like a shark attack. The last thing I remembered was the force of the oncoming car hitting me, and sensing what felt like every bone in my body implode into a million fragments. Everything went dark.

Elijah

WE WERE ALL ON STAND-BY in Emergency. Rainy days like these were always a foreboding omen of disaster, and already a horrific accident had occurred, and the police had called it through to us. I could hear the Doppler effect of the ambulance's wail drawing closer in the distance. It was going to be a long day.

I was the third to reach the ambulance. Hands started to push at me, pull me away. The babble of voices was confusing me, they made no sense; all I got from them was a staccato no, no, no. Then one word broke through – Lorien.

As the gurney trundled from the rear of the ambulance, I looked through the red and blue pulse of flashing lights illuminating the dreary morning in a gaudy cabaret effect. That broken body lying there, so still, so defeated... there was no way it could be my brother. But then, he opened his eyes and the surrealistic moment dissolved as I half lurched, half fell across to him. Again, the hands were grappling at me, dragging me away. Standing there, watching the gurney speed into the emergency corridor, my face reflected the agony that came with the pain of my shattered heart.

I raced in behind him. Outside the doorway into which they had taken him, their incessant hands once again shackled me. "Let me go!" I raged. Again, the muted mumblings were a distant drone. Finally, what seemed to be an hour later, Doctor Souter came through the door.

"Elijah... there is nothing we..." he started, but said no more. "He wants to see you," he finished softly. I elbowed my way into the room, sealing off the chaos as the door closed behind me.

Under the glow of fluorescent lighting, Lorien laid there, looking peaceful. I was too late! His eyes fluttered, then blinked open and he tried to smile. "Eli," he croaked, and I went to him. He raised a hand slightly, wanting me to take it, but it was bunched and unyielding, so I covered it with my own. Doctor Souter had sponged off his face, although the deep slashes told their own story and I looked down. The sheet that covered his grotesquely misshapen body was in bloom of reds and pinks. He shouldn't have still been alive. "Eli, listen to me." His words were mere breaths, so painful for him to even utter.

"I'm listening Lori," I whispered, knowing he had held on for just this reason.

"Paper, write..." A note, he wanted me to write a note. I grabbed my notepad and pen from the pocket of my white coat and sat closer, wanting to get every word. This was going to be for Mercy, for Ashlyn... Oh my God! Ashlyn! I shook the thought away and looked at him. He was but a blurry vision through my fresh onslaught of tears, and I wiped at them angrily, wanting to be able to see my twin fully.

"OK Lori, I'm ready." I had to lower my ear to his mouth to capture his final thoughts.

"I'm sorry... Baby, I don't want... to leave you... I'm sorry..." His thoughts were unfocussed, but I wrote them down verbatim. "Eli loves... you..., I want him...to love you... look after you ..."

"No Lorien," I said cutting him off, not able to believe the request he was making of Ashlyn, let alone of myself.

"Eli!" he rasped, exasperated. His breathing was becoming shallow, and I knew we were running out of time, so I humoured him, continuing to write. "Love him back... be the... family... we can no longer... be... I love you Baby... will be looking... out for you... always...

I will... love you...forever..." He stopped speaking and I looked down at him.

"Is that all?" I asked, and when he opened and closed his eyes twice in affirmation, I tossed the pad and pen aside, easing one arm up behind his head so I could hold him. His bunched hand reached for my own again and I cupped it. This time it relaxed, and something fell into my palm. I moved my hand out from under his and looked into it; a pendant lay there glinting in the light. During that one second of distraction, Lorien died in my arms.

Sitting there in the staff room, a cup of something hot clutched between my interlaced hands, Doctor Souter put his hand over my knee and I looked up at him. "Do you want me to make some calls for you?" he offered. I shook my head.

"No, I'll ring Mum and Dad before I leave, it's better that it comes from me." He nodded, understanding. Hellen walked in then, and passed a tray to Doctor Souter. "No!" I cried, "You are *not* sedating me!"

"OK Elijah, calm down. I thought you may have wanted it, maybe even for later." Thinking of later, I took the syringe and ampoule, pocketing them. I then asked to be alone. "Let me know when you are leaving," he said before he left the room.

My fingers didn't want to punch in Mum and Dad's number. How was I supposed to tell them? How was I supposed to tell Ashlyn? When I heard Mum's voice, I broke again into helpless sobs. "Elijah? Is that you?" Mum's voice sounded panicked, and I knew I had to speak.

"Mum," I started, not knowing what the next words were to be, "Lorien's dead." The words found themselves.

The ensuing fifteen-minute conversation was a blur. Dad got onto the extension and the three of us cried together. All I remember is telling them not to drive down, but to fly, and to call Anna and Dom, asking them to spread the word. I knew I couldn't keep making these calls.

And then there was nothing else I could do but go home.

I stuck my head into Doctor Souter's office on the way out, keeping my word on letting him know when I was leaving. "Do you want someone to drive you home Elijah?"

"No, it's not too far, and I need some thinking time." Doctor Souter knew Ashlyn and Lorien well, having delivered Mercy in this very hospital.

"Please call or text me when you arrive, so I know you are safe." I smiled weakly at him and he stood as I went to leave. "I thought you may want this," he said, his arm outstretched. For the second time in what seemed like mere seconds, something was dropped into my palm. This time, it was Lorien's diamond earring stud and wedding ring. Dr Souter hugged me fiercely, and my hug in return was weak and without hope.

All the way home in the car I battled within myself as to how I was going to break the news to Ashlyn. Lorien was dead; this was going to kill Ashlyn. Why in hell had I become a doctor?

All was quiet when I got home. I texted Doctor Souter then sat on the sofa, my head in my hands, wanting a few minutes of silence before I went in search of Ashlyn. She came bounding down the stairs before I had the chance. She stopped abruptly when she saw my face. "Elijah, what's happened?" she whispered, sitting next to me and taking my hands in her own. My hands still held the warmth of my brother's clutch, and I felt his final touch transferring to her.

"Lorien was in an accident," I said, my tears freshening. I pulled her close and whispered into her ear. "He died Ash," and I resumed the turbulent outburst. She lay still under my embrace, not moving. I didn't think she was even breathing, and I eventually drew back from her, taking her shoulders in my hands and looking into her eyes. She sat, zombie-like, then went to stand. "Where are you going?" I asked and pulled her back to the sofa.

"I need to get the washing out of the dryer." Her eyes were glassy, her voice that of a customer service voice robot. She was in shock.

"Ashlyn, look at me." She did, looking through me more than at me. I reached into my pocket and handed her the pendant, earring and ring. The landline rang and I glanced at it, deciding to let it ring. When I looked back to her, her face had crumpled into silent tears, her body heaving. I grappled her against me, and she found her voice, the loud wails and uncontrollable shudders physically rocking me with their strength. I did all I could do; let her cry and hold her.

When her exhausted sobs trickled into dry gasps, I lay her down on the sofa and went into the kitchen to get us something to drink. As I debated over tea or scotch, Ash's phone rang. It was Anna or Dom. "Hello."

"Oh Elijah," Anna wept, "I am so sorry! Does Ashlyn know?"

"Yes, do you want to talk to her?" I covered the mouthpiece and mouthed to Ash, *It's your mother.* She sat up and reached for the phone.

Whilst she spoke with her parents, I decided on tea with a shot of scotch. I reached into my coat to remove my mobile and other paraphernalia before taking it off, and the white sheet caught my eye. My God, did I give her Lorien's note? She would want to read his last thoughts, but considering what they contained, I had reservations in giving it to her. This was not my decision to make though, I realised; I had to consider my brother's last wishes. And I cried; cried at the unfairness of it all, cried for my loss, Ashlyn's, Mercy's, Mum and Dad's... Anna's, Dom's... the list was endless.

I didn't hear Ash finish the call; she was suddenly behind me, her hands wending around my waist. "What are we going to do Elijah? How can we live without him?" I sighed, finalising my decision, and pressed the note into her hands. "You read it to me," she said, sounding scared, passing it back to me. So I did.

Seconds later I turned quickly as I heard her hit the floor. The earlier tirade of emotion was nothing compared to this. Her wails had become near screams, her shuddering body now almost convulsing. I picked her up and held her in my arms, her small fists beating weakly against me. My broken heart cindered in response to her misery, but instead of crying into her, I reached for the syringe and filled it, jabbing her in the thigh. When she finally ebbed into half-sleep, I carried her upstairs and put her to bed. What else could I do?

I sat staring at the laptop through the stormy darkness, its LCD casting the only glow in the room. I felt like such a coward, but I didn't have the strength to call everyone, so decided on a blanket email instead. It would be hard for them to get the news this way, but I assumed they would understand.

I checked on Ashlyn before heading to bed. She lay quietly, the pendant in her hand, Lorien's wedding ring on her pointer finger. I took the pendant from her and draped it over the end bedpost where she would see it when she woke. A blaze of lightning cut through the afternoon in a blinding flash, illuminating the room. Her face saddened me so, crumpled up in an expression of such agony and defeat. I sat next to her, stroking her hair softly, wanting her to intake my soul through my touch, and give her some peace. The crack of ensuing thunder made me jump, so I left her and went back to my room, not wanting to disturb her fitful slumber. And then it was my turn to lose it…

It took me a long time to get to sleep, and I had never felt so alone in my life.

Ashlyn

WHEN I WOKE THE NEXT DAY, it was still raining, and hard. I sat watching through the dappled glass, studying the rivulets running their course, trickling into obscurity beyond the window's pane. I felt like I had the flu, my entire body aching, matching the pulse of my ever-slowing heart. And here I sat, waiting for it to finally cease pumping the blood through my body, wanting to put an end to this cotton-wool surround of nothingness. *Slower*, I willed it, *sloooower*. The rush of sound in my ears became increasingly muffled, making me smile. I had no need for a seashell to hear the faux waves within it, I was the influence on my own body, and I had it under my control. Not much longer now and my life force would solidify in my arteries, turning me into marble to match the pebble that was once my heart.

Yes, I was the famous Venus De Milo sculpture: hard, cold, timeless... armless. I had no need for meagre limbs, had no one to hold and cherish. The thickening black cloud of my mind was oozing through my body, taking me to the void I so desperately wanted to inhabit forever. It was such a lovely dream of an empty future, to be unaware of pain and misery. The breaths I took were shallow and ineffectual, and I closed my eyes, embracing the void, concentrating solely on it to keep away the other thoughts that wanted to force themselves into my mind.

I lay on the bed, waiting for it to be over. *Keep concentrating, don't think...* I slept.

The soft brush against my lips told me of Lorien's arrival. "Where have you been?" I whispered, and he silenced me, intensifying the kiss. Together we ascended into a womb of silence, drifting on the atmospheric tide, enveloped in each other. The material world fell away, and we soared through the darkness of the universe, it matching the passion and strength of our lovemaking. The starlight covered me, making my skin iridescent. Lorien reached out, plucking one from the night and tucked it behind my ear. His ethereal smile lit up my centre, making me exultant to be in his arms once more, to be loving him once more.

We were impossibly connected, every pore and cell in our bodies intertwined until we were a sole being, unknowing of where one of us ended and the other began. As Lorien glided through me, moving me across the inky expanse, the universe rolled and exploded into a brilliance of silver light. I closed my eyes and watched the world reform within my own internal darkness. The creation of the universe unfolded before me; comets flashed by, planets erupted, galaxies burst from nowhere into the abyss.

Lorien sealed his lips to mine, inhaling my final breath, and then raised me, his hands at my sides, throwing me into the radiance. "No!" I screamed, "Lorien no!" But he was waning, along with his smile. His fading hands scooped a luminous ball of sunshine from within his chest, blowing it to me like a milkweed kiss. As it hit and exploded through my body, I knew he had resided within me and my heart lurched, filling my soul with his warmth and essence. I reached the apex of Lorien's toss, looking down at him, reaching for him. He winked out of sight; I was then plummeting back to Earth, and I screamed.

"Ashlyn!"

The rocketing force with which I fell shook my body, rattled me in vibration that felt so very real. The molten ball he had thrown into my heart still burned intensely, keeping me warm.

"Ashlyn!!" My eyes flew open, disoriented, until my eyes locked with Elijah's. He was shaking me. "Babe, you were screaming..." He didn't get a chance to finish his thought as I burst into tears, letting the agony that I had contained like a festering boil, erupt. Lorien was dead.

I cried against Elijah and he held me tightly, trying to wring the torment from within me. My anguished sobs eclipsed his own; my trembling body outweighed the shudders I felt beneath my grasp. I finally looked up at him; the wet trail on his cheeks showed me that he too had been crying. Why wouldn't he have been? He had lost the ying to his yang; was now only a half-person, as was I. How could I be so damned selfish?

We held each other and let the misery drain from our souls until we were spent, exhausted. I caught his gaze and gave him a watery smile. There was no need for words; we both knew exactly how each other was feeling without the need to speak. "You need to eat something," Elijah murmured, pressing his lips against my brow.

"Always the doctor," I teased, and he smiled at me. We both then went downstairs to eat.

"So, talk to me Ash, you need to express how you're feeling. It may sound like crap advice at the moment, but it will help," Elijah offered.

"I feel dead inside."

"Yeah, I know."

"Yes, you do know, you are the only one who knows how I feel," I sighed.

"No, not really Ash. I haven't lost a husband, and not even in the more common way of illness or old age. No one knows what you are going through, not even me."

"But you have your own side to it Elijah; I haven't lost my twin. Therefore, I can't compare my loss to yours either." He smiled wanly at me; we certainly were a matching pair of morose bookends. "I don't think I will ever feel... will ever be able to get past this," I said, the fat tears forming on my lids briefly, before skittering down my face again. "I'm empty inside and can't imagine life without him."

Elijah came and sat next to me, taking me in his embrace. "He was such a major part of our lives Ash."

"You have to help me Elijah," I begged, grasping his shirt in my hands and looking at him with pleading eyes. "You have to make this go away!"

"Shhh," he soothed, running his hand comfortingly over my back. "There is only time Babe, only time... One day you will wake up and think of Lori with a smile and not a tear. And then, eventually you will laugh at some of his memories instead of being tormented by them."

"I can't imagine it," I mumbled, my face pressed back against him.

"It seems impossible right now, but it will come to pass... with time." We sat in silence for the longest time, and I allowed the warmth of him to soothe me, trying to draw his strength into myself.

My mobile rang, and I lamentably drew away. It was Michael; I managed a small smile. "Hi Michael."

"How are you doing chick? Stupid question I suppose."

"Yeah, well, you know..."

"Can we come and see you?"

"You don't ever need to ask that, Michael; you guys are always welcome." I could hear the smile in his voice.

"Thanks Ash. I just spoke to your mother. Thought I would check before I rang you, and Mercy wants to come home."

"Would you mind picking her up on your way over?"

"That's another reason why I'm calling; thought I would save you the trip."

"That would be wonderful Michael, thanks. See you soon then?"

"That you will. I love you Ash."

"I love you too Michael."

As I hit the end-call button, I looked at Elijah who had a smile on his face. "Looking forward to seeing them too?" I asked before I sniffed, and grabbed a tissue, wiping my runny nose.

"Well yes, but you have my shirt creases indented on your face," he said and laughed. I ran a hand over my cheek and felt the furrowed lines, wondering how long we had sat against each other in one frozen position. I smiled, then laughed. It felt good and I never thought I would ever feel the emotion of laughter again, especially not eighteen hours after I had lost my world. This thought made me break into instant uncontrolled tears; I was like a tap. Elijah wrapped his arm around me and led me into the bathroom, allowing me to slow the ebb and freshen up before our friends arrived. I also didn't want to be howling in front of Mercy; she would be confused enough.

Final words from Michael

"CAN YOU ANSWER THAT," I called to Glen, hearing the phone buzzing. I was currently elbow-deep in sudsy dishwater. I didn't really pay much attention to the conversation, going back to scrubbing the particularly stubborn skillet. The sudden lengthy silence eventually caught my attention, and I turned to Glen, eyebrows raised.

"I'll put him on." Glen looked up at me as he brought me the phone, his eyes pooling with tears.

"What's wrong?" I asked, wiping my hands quickly on my jeans before taking it from him.

"Oh Michael…" he started, but no other words would come. I went cold as I put the phone to my ear, thinking something had happened to my mother. My lips were like petrified wood, not joined to my face, as I said,

"Hello?" My voice sounded distant, as if coming from another room.

"Hello Michael, it's Anna," Ashlyn's Mum answered. My knees went to jelly, and I sat hard on the kitchen floor. I knew instantly that this conversation was about to change my life. "I have some bad news…" I hadn't spoken, hadn't commented to Anna, but she knew I was still here and waiting on the worst.

As she conveyed the news from yesterday, and how it had happened, my thoughts became unfocussed and wild. My emotions were fighting each other, from panic to anarchy, denial to a degree of sorrow I never thought I would feel, could feel. I listened until she was finished, and still without speaking, hit the end-call button, putting the phone carefully on the floor beside me. I was in slow motion; I was doing all the usual actions in life with the methodical deliberation they didn't deserve. But, by maintaining this control over myself, it could mean that with some careful thought, I could solve this problem. Either make it go away, or reverse time… Anything was possible right? "Michael," Glen said. "Michael!" again, but more forcefully. I couldn't move my eyes. I couldn't move at all. My ears were the only thing that seemed to be working, and I didn't want to hear anything more. Anna's news was enough to last me a lifetime. If I were to be struck deaf this very instant, I would rejoice. And in the dark, rear part of my mind, I felt fear. A fear so great, knowing I was about to be the strongest friend I could ever possibly be. Was I strong enough? The Cher song leapt into my head and I barked out a crazy laugh.

All my life I had portrayed myself as a confident man. And, it wasn't that I doubted the belief in myself, oh no, not at all. Before 'coming out of the closet', before I became my true, proud, gay self, I had gone through the same sense of failure as a teen that I supposed we all did. My brash exterior and flippant attitude though had concealed a lot of the confidence issues I had. Ashlyn knew me; knew me so well that she would have seen through this, as would have Bree and possibly even Simon. They would all be relying on me to be the strength of our group and find the words, be the rock. I didn't think I could do it. But, I also didn't have a choice.

I sensed more than saw Glen shift down beside me on the floor. He took my hand, a hand made of plasticine and glue. No warmth touched any of my limbs; no feeling resided within me at all. I was an empty vessel. "Michael, you're in shock," I heard Glen through the tunnel of fog. No, I didn't think I was. I simply understood I was not man enough to be the friend to Ashlyn that she would need of me, and I had never felt so terrified of anything in my life. I also had to collect Mercy and take her home. All I wanted to do though was to curl into a ball and go to sleep. A sleep to go on into eternity.

I scared myself even further when I felt the growing sensation in my chest. I thought I was going to have a heart attack, so intense it was, and with a lurch, my stupor broke, and I threw my head back and howled. As it abated, the tears burst from my eyes, my hands bunched into fists, which repeatedly found the floor. BANG, BANG, BANG. Was I going insane? I was not in control of this, and without concern, allowed it, for once, to happen.

Glen let me be, letting me rage at the world through sightless eyes and senseless ramblings. And eventually, when my energy had ebbed from its peak, he drew his arms around me and held me to him. I had no idea of how long we sat like that, but it seemed forever.

Eventually, the bubble of perspective popped us from our trance. I knew I had to get my shit together. I looked up at Glen, who was already focussed on me. "I know I haven't known them as long as you..." he started, but I cut him off.

"That is irrelevant Glen. This is bigger than that. I don't have to tell you how this is going to change our lives, and the environment that governs us all." Glen nodded, he understood. "I have to pick Mercy up on the way over to Sommersett."

"Does she know?"

"Yes, Anna and Dom have told her, but she doesn't understand."

"This will be hard on her," Glen noted.

"This will be hard on us all," I added, in almost a whisper.

When we arrived in Warden, Mercy ran out to greet us, in the same manner she always did. No, she did not understand. "Unkie Michael, Unkie Glen!" she called and ran at me, stopping only when she hit my legs, wrapping her little arms around them. "My Daddy is dead," she announced, looking up at me. I reached down for her, and hoisted her onto my hip. There was nothing I could say to this, so I pressed her face into my neck, crying against her. When my sobs became more intense, I felt Glen taking her from me. Looks like he was initially going to be the strong one for both of us. "Why is Unkie Michael crying?" I heard her ask.

"Because he is going to miss your Daddy," he explained, then added, "and is sad for how your mother will be feeling."

"Why is Mummy sad?" And, Glen answered, in the only way she may understand,

"Because your Daddy is dead." She still didn't get it though. In time, she would.

I rang their house before leaving Warden, for two reasons: to scope out how my reaction would be, and to speak to Ash before seeing her. This was all new territory for me, and I was doing my best. She sounded OK in comparison to how I was feeling. A flush of guilt and shame suddenly raced through me, outweighing the self-pity I was feeling for myself. How could I be so worried about my involvement in all of this when an entire family had been sent through the cyclone belt?

Elijah answered the door on our arrival, and I didn't speak, didn't know what to say, so simply took him in my arms. Eventually he drew back, rubbing a hand across his sodden eyes. "Ash is upstairs if you want to go up and see her." I didn't, but I went anyway.

I knocked softly on the door. If she failed to respond, I would slink away like the coward I was, but a soft, "Come in," floated out to me.

Again, I felt like I was moving in slow motion. As I snicked the door shut behind me, I turned to face my best friend. She was lying on the bed, and moved onto her side, patting the bed, beckoning me to sit beside her. I took her hand as I sat on the bed, and then broke into tears again.

Several minutes later when I realised she was comforting me, I managed to regain my composure, and responsibility, and smiled feebly at her. "I'm supposed to be providing you with comfort, not the other way around," I sniffed.

"It's like the end of my world, Michael," she confided, then smiled widely, surprisingly. "He called to me Michael, he was with me." I wasn't sure to what level I believed in the afterlife, not sure whether she was medicated, and also not sure of whether she was losing it. It all came down to how she felt about the afterlife I supposed, and whether it gave her some peace. It certainly appeared to.

She went into detail of the experience, his voice calming; she felt his touch, he held her. "I hope I can call on him when I need to," she finished with a sigh, and dropped back into my arms.

"You're exhausted, I think you should get some sleep," I suggested, happy in the knowledge I was being sincere. My previous, selfish concerns had disappeared now I was with her. I had found my strength again.

"OK. Are you going to be here for a while?"

"Yes, and Simon and Bree will be here this afternoon." Simon was in Sydney at a conference when Anna rang him with the news; Bree was home, and waiting for him.

"And is Mercy here?"

"Yes, she's downstairs with Glen and Elijah."

"Oh, good," she answered quietly, then drifted off to sleep.

Glen and I picked up Cara and Nick at Castlebrook airport that afternoon, glad there was something we could be doing for the family as a whole. I remembered all too clearly when Nick lost his mother, the twins their beloved Nanna, and how it had affected them. Not knowing whether they wanted you there for support, whether you were under their feet, whether you were saying and doing the right things, or making it worse. There was no manual to follow when it came to death, and when it was a member of the family taken so tragically, and so young, it was even more obscure.

Cara and Nick both looked like a wrung-out old dishrag. A lot of tears had been shed, and possibly they had also not slept since they received the news. Poor Elijah, how had he been able to call them, and then, more sorrowfully, to have to tell Ashlyn? I admired him so much. His strength in the face of adversity was unfathomable. I doubted I would have been able to cope as well, however, when faced with the issue, I suppose it has to be done. It was so very selfish of me even to think it, but I hoped that I would never have to understand the emotion of what Elijah had to go through.

Talk was limited during the car ride home, but it was a united comfortable silence. They were also anxious to see their son and to comfort as only loving parents can. They asked how all three of them were going, and we explained Mercy was unaware of the depth this change in their life meant. In time though, when her Daddy didn't come home, she would grasp the greatness of the pain. How sad that she had to learn such a harsh lesson so young. It was so unfair.

Elijah met us at the door, and Cara took him straight into her arms, with Nick then encompassing them both. Their bodies, melded as one, shuddered under the force of their tears. Glen and I dissolved into the kitchen to put the kettle on, although a stiff drink was probably more of a requirement. We could hear their muted conversation when they finally broke apart and the strength of their love for their children, their twin, brought me to fresh tears. Glen took me in his arms and let me cry, thankful of the kitchen barrier-wall that hid my grief from a family so consumed with their own. They didn't need to see me adding to it.

Eventually, Cara came into the kitchen. With me still crying, she took me in her arms. "Oh Mrs Standish, please forgive me for being so upset. I can't imagine how it must feel for you all; and here I am making it even worse!"

"Dear, sweet Michael," she started, drawing slightly away to look up into my eyes, wiping the tears from my cheeks softly with her thumbs. With my face in her hands, she continued, "You have nothing to apologise for. This affects us all and in so many ways. To see you like this confirms how much the world loved my son; my sons," she corrected herself. I nodded, not able to speak for fear of bursting into a fresh tirade.

Eventually, Elijah took his parents up to Ashlyn. Again, it was so selfish of me, but I was glad I wasn't witness to that. I then thought of Mercy. Where was she? I found her in the corner of the rumpus room, hunkered down behind the piano, colouring. She looked like a timid deer, unsure of what was going on around her. The adults she knew and loved so well were not acting the way they should be. I knelt down to her height and she looked at me, her face flushed. I opened my arms to her, and she threw herself against me. She wasn't crying, she didn't know the devastation yet, but her little body was hot and shuddering. So confused.

I held her until a knock came at the door. Glen opened it, and Bree and Simon were standing there. I motioned to Mercy, and Simon and Bree managed to hold themselves together. I don't know how they did it. Glen spoke with them quietly for a few seconds, then came over to Mercy and me. "How about a Happy Meal at McDonalds?" Glen asked Mercy brightly.

"Yay!" she responded, and skipped to the door, hugging her Uncle Simon, then Aunty Bree around the legs. Again, I don't know how they managed to keep it together; we hadn't even had a chance to talk yet. It was near dinner time though and everyone may possibly be getting hungry, so it was a great idea to get out of the house to allow the Standish's some time alone, and we would bring dinner back for them once we could prise Mercy off the play gym.

The whirlwind of the next few days went past in a blur. Ash and Mercy did not go to the funeral; Mercy in fact was staying with Anna and Dom for the moment. They picked her up from Ashlyn after the service, not staying for the wake. They had been Ash's rock, but so quietly involved. Their love of their only child, only daughter, knew no boundaries, especially when it came to being her life-support.

Lorien's memory was immortalised through his songs being played, which created glowing smiles on so many faces. This was the glory of a wake; the ability to smile through tears at the wonderful memories of those you hold so close in your heart. But, this wasn't something I wanted to think about too much. It was like a knife plunging repeatedly into my heart. Each time, the memory of the day wanted to take over my thoughts.

You look into your past every now and then, remembering the things that made you laugh and cry, cringe or stand proud. Then you stop and evaluate your present – your here and now. How the things in your past forged you into the person you are today. Whether that is humble, joyful, knowing how to love, knowing how to react to what encroaches your 'you' space. Whether 6, 16, 26 or 96, it's our past that sculpts who we are in our present. And then, you look into the future, and think… what's next?

THE END

EPILOGUE

I WASN'T IN A VERY GOOD PLACE for a long time after Lorien died. I didn't go to the funeral, as much as my friends and family had gently persuaded me to. They thought I would regret it at some later stage in my life, but there was no need for me to be there. All of those faces looking at me with such sadness; making me the centre of attention on a day where I would want to be invisible. It was an empty ceremony anyway; Lorien was not at that service any more than I was. He was in my heart, and that's where he would always be. Perhaps it was selfish of me, but at the time, I really didn't care.

Mum and Dad took Mercy for an initial couple of weeks to give me some grieving time. I didn't do much over this period, watched the walls more than anything, trying to hear his voice calling me, to capture one last blissful vision. He never called again, but I called him.

It was Elijah who got me to the final stage where I stopped watching back our DVDs and flicking through our wedding albums on a daily basis. It was also he who reminded me how pissed off Lorien would be with me for being so depressed, and not having our little girl in our home with me. Elijah missed her too.

A fortnight later, when Mercy came home, Cara and Nick decided it was time to leave. Elijah and his parents were a wonderful support for me, and I didn't think I could have managed without them. Elijah especially tended to my every need, and eventually took a few months off working at Dr Wood's surgery to be with me as a carer and friend. I myself went onto an unknown period of leave without pay from work, and to be able to spend each day together as a family was a soothing balm, which assisted in helping to heal us all. But oh, so slowly…

But time didn't stand still for any reason and it was now nearly six months since Lorien's death. I had turned twenty-seven in July, and our little girl was nearly four. I was amazed at how quickly time flies when you have a little one growing up around you. When she did things occasionally, things that were so like the way her father would have done them, I found myself looking upward and thinking, *Are you watching Lorien? Can you see our little girl? I miss you...* I tried to keep these to a minimum however and it was still so painful, and would probably always be that way.

It was coming up to the first Christmas without Lorien and it had been just as hard as the day he died. I was watching Mercy playing with her building blocks, assisted by Unkie Lie, that I had a silent tear. I had learnt how to rein these tears in mostly, and although still with a heavy heart, I had pulled myself together enough to go on with life – for her sake primarily. But every time I looked into my baby girl's eyes, I saw her father looking back at me. It was a wonderful thing, but such a painful thing, knowing she would never truly understand the strength of his love for her, and me. It made my heart break.

Mercy had started calling Elijah 'Daddy' a while back, which made us both smile, made us happy. If this was how she managed to comprehend her new situation, how to deal with it, who were we to stop it? It was still hard to hear though, as she had only called Lorien 'Daddy' a handful of times before he was killed, killed crossing that damn road.

I had no interest in dating or seeing anyone else, although Michael and Bree had tried. They would have had impossibly large shoes to fill, and it would only get as close as being an ill-fitted size by another pair of Standish feet. I had battled with Lorien's last words to me for a long, long time. I knew he had been sincere, knew I would be taken care of by someone he believed to have loved me nearly as much as he did. I also knew how hard it would have been for Elijah to deliver his last words to me via a handwritten note, knowing what it contained. *Eli loves you Baby, please, let him take care of you... I will love you forever.* Forever is what we were supposed to have had; forever was bullshit.

I swiped at my tears in anger, I didn't mean to have found myself in this sad place, but it came upon me without warning at times and there was little I could do about it. I still loved him and still felt so cheated that he was out of my life. This is where Elijah found me, sitting on the floor of my bedroom, crying. I felt so stupid when I felt his hand on my shoulder, leaning down to take my hand and stand me with him, hugging me warmly in comfort. I had done my share of comforting him too when I came out of the fog. He had lost his twin and that was something he had with Lorien well before I came on the scene. He drew my face back and I smiled at him through my tears. "I'm OK, just having another Lorien moment." He wiped his fingers across my cheeks and kissed me on the forehead.

"Mercy is looking for you, she has something to show you," he said and embraced me once more, rubbing his hand over my back.

"Where is she?" I didn't need to ask as I heard a trundling of running feet and she burst through the door, clinging to both Elijah and me.

"Mummy, come with me, I have to show you something!" Elijah smiled at me and took my hand, leading me downstairs to the lounge room as Mercy raced ahead.

"Wow!" I rightfully exclaimed when I saw the crayoned work of art waiting for me on the dining room table. "Is this you, me and Daddy?"

"Yes, both of them," she said, motioning to the brunette man standing on my other side in the drawing, with long brown curls, so much like her own. Mercy was on Elijah's shoulders and Lorien, Elijah and I were all holding hands.

"Well, you have managed to make both of your daddies as handsome as they are in real life." Elijah rolled his eyes at me and sat, pulling Mercy up onto his knee. He played a kiss to the back of her hair and she twisted suddenly to kiss his cheek before returning to her excited chatter.

"And that's Nanny and Poppy Standish, and Grandma and Grandpa," she pointed out. Although overcome at times with sudden grief, I still had a little family, which had brought me back to life. Of this I was glad, and I bent down to kiss her before going to start dinner.

GLOSSARY OF AUSSIE SLANG

- All over red rover: to announce the end of something, ie a game, marriage, etc.
- Boardies: abbreviation of board-shorts. Knee length quick drying swim shorts, worn by all sexes, but predominantly males.
- Bucketed down: Poured down with heavy, soaking rain.
- Bullshitting: lying.
- Busted: caught in the act, guilty.
- Canteen: snack bar. Also known in Australia as a tuck-shop. Where food and drinks can be bought, often run by mothers of the students. No formal seating is in place, but rows of benches are often located outside of the canteen. Canteens are also found at local sporting grounds.
- Centimetres: 1 inch = 2.54 centimetres.
- Chocolate Crackles: Similar to what is called 'rice crispy treats' in the USA, however Chocolate Crackles have cocoa powder, no marshmallow, and are put into cupcake patties and eaten individually.
- Chips: fries. But this is where it can get confusing, we also refer to potato crisps as chips. If someone were to ask you to pass them a packet of chips, you could well be given a packet of Doritos and that would be totally acceptable.
- Cockhead: see dickhead.
- Cocktail frankfurts: little weenies or little hotdogs. Finger sized frankfurts.
- Cordial: a concentrated sweet syrup to be mixed with water before consumption.
- Cut and dried: clear and definite. Not needing much thought or discussion.
- Dickhead: fool, idiot. Never meant in a nice way. A wanker or cockhead is a 'bigger dickhead' and a 'fuckwit' is the biggest and worst of them all. A smart-arse is of a similar level to a dickhead, but they are usually arrogant, smug and a know it all, moreso than a fool or idiot.
- Dodgem cars: bumper cars.

- Ermagerd: 'oh my God'.
- Esky: portable cooler, cooler box, ice box, chilly-bin, igloo.
- Fairy bread: buttered slices of white bread covered in 'hundreds and thousands', or 'sprinkles' as they are known in the USA.
- Fairy floss: cotton candy, candy floss.
- Finger (give the): flipping the bird. Using the middle finger to give an obscene hand gesture.
- Full-blown: to the maximum extent of, the nth degree.
- Full bore: maximum effort.
- Goss: short for gossip.
- Heaps: a lot, plenty.
- Jelly: a gelatine based dessert, known as jello in the USA.
- Kilometre: 1 kilometres = 0.62 miles
- Lemonade: What the US would call 'Sprite'. Sprite is a brand in Australia. The Aussie lemonade is a clear, carbonated, colourless soft drink, barely represented by lemons. Lemon squash, or pub squash, or squash is the Australian equal of the USA (cloudy) lemonade.
- Lollies: candy.
- Meat pie: is a hand-sized pastry containing diced or minced meat and gravy, sometimes with onion, mushrooms, bacon, or cheese and often consumed as a take-away food snack. Similar to a pot pie. The meat pie is considered iconic in Australia and can be purchased at every bakery, sporting ground canteen and other outdoor events. Great with heaps of tomato sauce.
- Mob: group.
- Oi!: rhymes with boy. Means hey! It gets someone's attention.
- Packed: as in 'it's too packed'. Crowded.
- Pass the parcel: a children's game at parties where a parcel is passed around to music. When the music stops the child holding the 'parcel' gets to remove a layer of wrapping, hoping to find a treat. The final removal of the wrapping will hold a prize, like a toy.
- Pigs in a blanket: a finger food served cold at parties. It is a mashed potato tube wrapped in a slice of devon (baloney).

- Pissed / pissed at / pissed off: to be cranky or angry. 'He pissed me off'. 'I'm pissed at him', 'I'm pissed that we had to miss out'. For drunk, see also 'write yourself off'.
- Plasticine: a children's putty-like modelling clay. Similar to play-doh.
- Pluto pup: corndog. Also known as a Dagwood dog in Australia. This is a frankfurt (red hotdog) on a stick, covered in batter and deep fried. Great with tomato sauce!
- Pretty much: just about.
- Rashies: a sun protective SPF T-shirt styled top worn when swimming or surfing. Children will wear them on any occasion when out in the sun.
- Reckon: think, as in - What do you reckon? What do you think?
- Rissoles: are very similar to a burger pattie or meatball, and is made from minced meat without a pastry covering. Aussie rissoles are round and often barbecued or fried, and eaten as part of a meal with either salad in summer, or vegetables in the cooler months.
- Sec: second. Not necessarily a literal meaning of one second. Hang on a sec could refer to as long as it takes, and definitely not only one second.
- Shush: quiet. Rhymes with push.
- Shy of: as in 'just shy of'. Just before. Can also refer to being 'just a little short' of, eg cash.
- Show (the): similar to a fair or carnival in the USA. They travel around Australia and visit a town annually.
- Showbag: (also known as sample bags) is a themed based bag of commercial and official merchandise. Similar to a 'goody bag', or a 'swag bag' in the USA. A person who 'looks good but is full of shit' (bullshitter) is also known as a showbag in Australia, due to the similarity of this person to an actual showbag itself.
- Shush: quiet. Rhymes with push.
- Sideshow alley: known as the midway in the USA.
- Smart-arse: see dickhead. Smart-arsed (as in grin): a very wide grin, usually showing smugness, self-satisfaction, or inner humour.
- Smashed: see 'write yourself off'.
- Snags: sausages.
- Tomato sauce: ketchup.

- Toothy pegs: teeth.
- Write yourself off: get really drunk, also 'smashed', 'paro' (as in paralytic), 'wasted', 'maggoted', 'hammered', 'pissed', ' blind'.
- Wuss: weak, cowardly or timid.
- Year 7: equivalent to USA first year of junior high (middle school).
- Year 8: equivalent to USA final year of junior high (middle school).

This glossary of Australian slang was developed to assist non-Aussies with any terms they find confusing in the novel. This could range from another country having a different understanding of the same word or phrase, to not understanding the term whatsoever.

The glossary outlines the reference to how the slang is used in the novel and is not all encompassing of every use of the word or phrase in Australia. Slang can also vary from state to state, which is why immigrants who have lived here for decades still look at we born and bred Aussies in total confusion when we speak. Who can blame them! ☺

A special thank you to my dear friend Jennifer D McLaughlin, my USA mate and pen-pal since we were 13 years old. Her input into this glossary from an American perspective has been immeasurable. Thanks Jen!

About the author

Cassandra Ann Frew (nee Souter) was born on a July winter's night in Hornsby NSW. At the age of three, the family moved to a dairy farm outside Lismore NSW where she spent the majority of her childhood. At ten years old, the family moved to Lake Macquarie NSW.

Cassie found her love of romance writing during her high school years, and her first several 'novels' were hand-written exercise books, passed around for her friends to read.

Her career in business and administration has led her into further self-education including web design, IT, professional proofreading and editing, creative writing and industrial psychology. She is also a Justice of the Peace and a Civil Celebrant.

Her most rewarding achievement to date is what she has in common with the residents of the Standish household – their love of music, playing an instrument and the 80s. What a decade!

These stories belong to my readers, and to Ashlyn and the Standish family. This is how love should be, can be, is.